BLOOD IN THE
WATER

SHERRYL D. HANCOCK

VULPINE
PRESS

Published by Vulpine Press in the United Kingdom in 2018

ISBN 978-1-83919-269-2

Cover by Claire Wood

www.vulpine-press.com

Also in the *MidKnight Blue* series:

CHAPTER 1

Susan was looking for Midnight. She had called the department and been told by Cassandra Devereaux that Chief Chevalier-Debenshire had taken the morning off. She called Rick and Midnight's house and was surprised when Rick answered on the third ring. He sounded very relaxed. Susan had no idea that as she spoke to her uncle he was grinning down at his wife. He lay over her still after having made love to her. They had been lazily discussing whether to go into the office or stay in bed until Mikeyla got home from school.

"Uncle Rick?" Susan said hesitantly. She was surprised that he was home—maybe something was wrong. "Is everything alright?"

Rick laughed, his voice sounding very mellow. "Yes, Susan, everything's fine. What's up?"

Midnight watched him, her catlike eyes glittering with subdued humor.

"I was looking for Midnight, and I was told that she was off this morning. Is she there?"

"Yeah, she's here," Rick said smoothly. "Hold on."

It was obvious to Susan that Midnight was very close, since she came on the line almost immediately.

"Hey, Susan, what's up?" Midnight said, sounding much like Rick had. Susan began to wonder if she'd interrupted something.

"Is this a bad time?" Susan asked, chagrined.

Midnight smiled on her end of the line as Rick moved to lie next to her, his hand on her waist. "A few minutes ago would have been a bad time—now's fine," she said, almost laughing at the look Rick gave her. He made a face, rolling his eyes to indicate that she hadn't needed to tell his niece that much.

"Oh…" Susan said, not sure how to respond.

"Don't worry about it. What's up?" Midnight asked again, grinning as Rick started to kiss her shoulder and then moved down her arm. She turned over on her side with her back to him, the phone cradled between her ear and the pillow under her head. She shivered as his lips moved to her waist, his hands sliding upward.

"I was wondering," Susan was saying, "if you were free for lunch."

"Lunch?" Midnight echoed, feeling Rick shake his head. "Don't you have the kids today?"

"No, Randy took the day off from school. Joe's sick."

"Oh," Midnight said. "Yeah, I know he's sick. So she took the day off and gave you one, huh?"

"Yes, and I was hoping to talk to you, if I could, about some things."

Midnight glanced back at Rick, and he could see she was torn. He gave her a long look, pursing his lips then nodding to her. He figured he could talk her into coming home after lunch and finishing the day with him. After all, it was still only 9:00.

"Okay, how about eleven thirty?" Midnight said, smiling at her husband.

2

"Great," Susan said, sounding relieved.

"I'll pick you up."

"Okay, see you then."

After hanging up the phone, Midnight turned to her husband. "She sounds like she really needs to talk…"

"I figured as much by the way you looked," he said, leaning down to kiss her softly.

"Thanks for being cool about it."

"Yes, but," he said, placing a finger on her lips, "I want you to call the office and tell them you won't be in. And," he added before she could speak, "I want you back here right after lunch."

Midnight looked up at him, her green eyes narrowing as she grinned.

"Is that an order, Lieutenant?" she asked subserviently.

"As a matter of fact, yes, it is," he countered, his grin wide.

"Uh-huh." Midnight placed her hand on his shoulder and slid it down, trailing her nails across his chest, making him shudder.

"Uh-huh," he repeated, pulling her body flush with his and sliding his hand up to touch her breasts. Leaning down, he kissed her, his lips moving over hers sensually. Midnight moved her hands to entwine them in his hair. Within minutes they were both breathless and making love much as they did almost every day.

Afterward, they lay together trying to catch their breath. He was next to her, his leg thrown over hers possessively, still stroking her skin with his hand. Midnight lay on her back, her left arm still over his, her hand still in his hair, caressing his back.

3

"So how come we don't do this more often?" Midnight asked, her voice still showing the effects of their lovemaking.

"Because you have a department to run, and I have a unit," he said softly.

"Oh yeah." Midnight nodded, then grinned. "But this is still nice…"

He smiled. "Yes, it is. Maybe we need to think about another vacation. We haven't had one since you made chief. Maybe you need a break."

"Maybe…" Midnight said, closing her eyes. She was surprised when he woke her a little while later.

"Night," he whispered, his lips close to her ear. "Baby, it's ten forty-five. Do you want me to call Susan and cancel?" He'd been loath to wake her, she'd been sleeping so peacefully. He'd been watching her for an hour.

Midnight shook her head, snuggling a little bit closer to him. "No, I'm going. When did I fall asleep?"

"'Bout an hour ago," he said, grinning. "Guess I'm just not stimulating company."

"Oh, you're stimulating all right," she said assuredly. "Maybe too much—you wore me out." She grinned, reaching up to touch his cheek. "And I'll be back for more after lunch."

Rick smiled, shaking his head. "The things I have to do to keep you happy…" He trailed off as she pushed him back on the bed. She sat up, leaning over him to look into his eyes.

"I'm crazy about you, you know," she said, her voice very serious.

4

"Yeah?" he replied, his voice equally so. "Well, I'm kinda gone over you myself."

She smiled at him, and he returned it. Reaching up, he brushed her hair over one bare shoulder. Midnight leaned down and kissed him, her eyes never leaving his.

"I gotta take a shower," she said a couple of minutes later. She got off the bed and headed for their bathroom. Rick watched her go, astounded once again by how beautiful his wife was. At thirty-four she was still as beautiful and wild as she had been the day they met. Her copper-blond hair still reached almost to her waist, because he'd threatened her with great bodily harm if she cut it. Her body was still lean and strong, especially since she'd taken up jogging on the beach most mornings. She told him it helped her to clear her head for the day's events.

It was Rick's opinion she'd been overdoing it for months, and he figured her fatigue now was a sure sign that she needed a break. He made a mental note to himself to look into getting away soon. It wasn't as easy for him to do as it had been before. Now that he ran FORS, he had begun to realize what Midnight had dealt with for years, and why she was never able to just take a day or two off without ramifications. As it was, he knew that by playing hooky one day, his desk would be extra loaded the next day. It was worth it to him, to spend time with her. He had never been able to get over how much he loved her. His feelings ran so deep it was hard to discern where his love for her stopped and his own self-preservation began, they were so intertwined.

Twenty minutes later, Midnight emerged from the bathroom and got dressed. Her hair was still damp as she leaned down to kiss him.

"Shouldn't you dry your hair?" he asked, sounding like a father.

"I don't have time. I don't want Susan to feel like she's messed up our day. Otherwise I'll never get anything out of her," she said, laughing at the last.

Rick laughed too. He knew how shy his niece could be generally—when she thought she was out of line, she could be impossible to deal with.

"Then you better get goin', Chief," he said mildly.

"Yes, sir," she replied sharply, as a cadet would.

Midnight pulled up to Joe and Randy's house twenty minutes later; she was five minutes early. She stopped in to check on her long-time partner before she and Susan left.

"So, old man, how's it going?" Midnight asked as she walked into Joe and Randy's family room.

Joe was lying on the couch, his head on Randy's lap, with her hands as usual in his hair. He looked up, his light blue eyes narrowing at Midnight.

"Watch it, little girl. I can still kick your ass, pneumonia or not," he said, his tone mockingly threatening.

"Yeah, yeah." Midnight waved away his threat with a delicate hand. "So it is pneumonia, huh?"

Randy nodded. "The doctor said we caught it early though."

"Yeah," Joe put in. "I should be back to full strength by tomorrow."

"More like Wednesday or Thursday," Randy said authoritatively.

Midnight nodded, giving Joe a knowing look. "You listen to your wife, Sinclair. She's the one with the brains in the family."

Joe grinned. "Thanks."

"Anytime," Midnight said, smiling widely.

"Okay, so I have pneumonia. What's your excuse?" Joe said, his tone changing just slightly. Midnight easily picked up on the concern.

"What are you trying to say, Sinclair?" she replied indignantly.

"I'm sayin' that you look like you could use about a week's worth of sleep," Joe said, ever protective.

"I'm alright," she said dismissively. "Just need to get about thirty hours into a twenty-four-hour day, that's all."

"Slow down," he said sternly. "The bad guys aren't going to leave town, ya know?"

Midnight grinned at him. "It really isn't a big deal. I think I might be getting the flu Keyla had last week."

Joe nodded, not totally believing her but knowing arguing with her was moot. She always did her own thing regardless of how many people tried to look out for her.

Once in the car, Midnight looked over at Susan but said nothing. She started toward a Mexican restaurant near the beach. On the drive they talked about trivial things—Joe and Randy's kids, school, the department. Midnight knew Susan would get around to bringing up what was bothering her eventually.

Susan waited until they were seated at the restaurant and had ordered. The window they sat next to had a very nice view of the beach, about a quarter of a mile down below.

"Aunt Midnight, how long did you know my uncle before you knew you loved him?" she asked, watching her with eyes so much like Rick's.

Midnight considered the question for a long moment, not sure how to answer it.

"I mean," Susan said, seeing Midnight's hesitation, "did you know right away or did it take a while?"

"It took a while," Midnight said. "With us, everything was all fire and ice. It took a long time to get past that so we could fall in love."

"But you did fall in love," Susan said. It was a statement; she knew they loved each other.

"Yes, we did," Midnight replied, her smile enigmatic.

"But you had sex long before that."

Midnight grinned. "Oh yes. But I've always been of the opinion that my heart and my sex drive are in two different places, and they don't always have to be in sync."

"Yes," Susan said, seizing on Midnight's statement almost desperately. "So it's possible that someone you don't love can excite you and it doesn't have to mean anything, right?"

Midnight thought about it for a minute, then nodded. "Yeah, I guess so. I mean, in the beginning, Rick and I would be fighting one minute and making love the next. And that was before I loved him— he just really made me crazy sometimes."

"Why?" Susan asked, ever fascinated by her uncle's relationship with his wife.

"Rick's as headstrong and stubborn as they come, and so am I. In the beginning, and even now sometimes, he wanted to control me, to make me do what he wanted me to do. I fought that, and still fight it, tooth and nail. It makes for a very lively relationship." Midnight said the last rolling her eyes.

"Lively," Susan repeated slowly. "Not rocky?"

"No," Midnight said firmly, shaking her head. "Rocky indicates there's a chance things will fall apart. Rick and I are together for good. We both know that now—that's what makes it okay to fight about stuff. Almost losing him once was enough to show me where I belong, and that's with him."

"But what if you're in love with someone," Susan said, her voice indicating the importance of what she was about to ask, "but that person doesn't excite you sexually. Will that change?" Susan's eyes begged Midnight to say yes, and Midnight knew they'd gotten to the real problem now.

"Things with Warren not going well?" she asked, avoiding Susan's question.

"Not what I expected, no," Susan said, her tone indicating her disappointment.

"Well, maybe it's just too soon."

"Did Rick excite you the first time?" Susan asked, her expression hopeful.

Midnight screwed up her face apologetically. "Yeah, he did. But you gotta realize, I've always been comfortable about sex, so that's kinda different. Warren's your first, isn't he?" Susan nodded. "Well,

9

maybe you just need to get comfortable with him before it will be good."

"I don't know…" Susan said, looking doubtful for reasons Midnight didn't understand. "You see, there's this other thing…"

"What other thing?" Midnight asked, furrowing her eyebrows.

Susan sighed heavily. "Christian Collins."

Midnight raised her eyebrows, her mouth dropping open. Then she started to grin conspiratorially. "What's going on with him?" she asked, her tone shocked.

Susan shook her head. "No, no, not *that*."

"But something?" Midnight asked hopefully.

"Well, yes… I mean, no…" Susan looked confused.

"Well, which is it?" Midnight asked, raising an eyebrow again. "Tell me what happened," she said when Susan looked hesitant.

"It was nothing, really." Susan looked out the window for a long moment, then back at her aunt. "He was sick and I brought him some medicine. He took it with alcohol and I was worried, so I stayed in his room to make sure he was okay. He slept and I watched. He doesn't have any chairs in his room so I ended up sitting on the bed next to him. The next thing I know his head is resting on me… then… well, he pulled me down next to him and put his arms around me and fell asleep again. I didn't know what to do. When I tried to move away he held me tighter. Then he put his face against my neck, and his lips touched me…" She trailed off, and Midnight knew she was thinking about it. "I swear, Midnight, my whole body lit up, but I got scared so I tried to move away again. Well, that woke him up. He taunted me, telling me not to get excited. And I told him that he

10

couldn't get me excited."

"Did he prove you wrong?" Midnight asked, her eyes twinkling.

"And how, I thought I'd die. I swear, he really didn't do all that much, I mean in terms of... you know..."

"How far did he go?" Midnight asked, trying to make it easier for Susan to give details without being too graphic.

"Only below the waist for about ten seconds, but that's what... you know."

"That's what did it?" Midnight was impressed. She'd figured Christian for being good in bed, but that good?

"Yes, and it's never felt like that with Warren, and he and I have gone so much farther than that." Susan sounded dismayed.

"So Christian turns you on," Midnight said, shrugging. "Who wouldn't be turned on by a guy that looks like that?"

"Yes, but..." Susan shook her head remorsefully. "What do I do about things with Warren? Does the fact that he doesn't turn me on mean something? I mean, how important is sexual attraction in a marriage?"

Midnight had to hold back her urge to snicker at the girl, knowing it would hurt her feelings. She took a deep breath instead, expelling it as she nodded. "To me it is. But maybe that's just me," she added lamely.

"Does Rick turn you on? I mean easily, like with a touch?" Susan was almost appalled that she was talking about her uncle this way, but curious at the same time.

Midnight gave her a deadpan look, her face very serious. "Susan, Rick can look at me in a certain way from across a room and it turns

11

me on."

"Really?" Susan looked shocked.

"Oh yeah," Midnight said, laughing. "You can imagine how disruptive that can be at the monthly staff meetings." She grinned, remembering well a few meetings that were cut short because she'd made eye contact with her husband and he'd given her *that* look. They laughed about it a lot, her lack of professionalism when it came to being in the same room with him when he was feeling amorous.

Susan laughed. "I never really thought of Uncle Rick that way, but I guess I could see it. My uncle is a handsome man."

"Oh yes," Midnight agreed. "And he's really good where it really counts." They both laughed then, and Midnight knew Rick would kill her if he knew they were talking about him like this. "I'll just bet that Christian's really good too…" she said, her voice taking on a mischievous tone.

"Well," Susan said, "he did tell me that what he had done was just the beginning of what he could make me feel…"

"Oh my God," Midnight said, widening her eyes dramatically even as she grinned outrageously. "He actually said that to you? And you didn't jump him right then and there?"

Susan rolled her eyes. "No, I'm a coward, remember?" She shrugged. "Besides, he followed it up by telling me that I had better leave before I got into more trouble than I could handle. I took his advice."

Midnight gave her a pointed look. "Well, maybe next time you shouldn't."

"What do you mean? Sleep with him?" Susan was aghast at the

thought.

"Well, not necessarily him, but definitely with someone else. If you aren't sure about Warren, slow things down. Nothing says you can't back up a bit. Even give back the ring for a while to see other people."

Midnight knew Rick would be pissed about her encouraging Susan to break it off with Warren. Their opinions on this subject differed significantly. But Midnight was adamant about one thing—she didn't want Susan marrying this man because everyone else thought it was right. She wanted her to marry the man that Susan herself thought was right.

"But what will happen if Warren won't marry me then? If he changes his mind?" Susan asked tremulously.

"Babe, if he changes his mind that easily, then he's not right for you anyway," Midnight said, almost sharply.

"I guess you're right," Susan said, but her voice still indicated her concern.

"Hey." Midnight put her hand over Susan's, looking into the younger woman's eyes. "You don't have to do anything. I just want you to be happy with your choice for a husband. What do you want out of this?"

Susan was quiet for a long moment as she thought about it. "I want what you and my uncle have, or what Randy and Joe have, something like that."

Midnight nodded, reflecting on the difference between her and Rick's relationship and Randy and Joe's relationship, but understanding what Susan meant.

"That's what I want for you too," she said.

Susan nodded sadly. "And you don't think I'll have that with Warren?"

Midnight thought about it for a minute. "Let me ask you something. How long does it take for you to miss him?"

"What?"

"When he drops you off, when you leave school and him at the end of the day. How long does it take not seeing him till you miss him?"

"I don't know," Susan said, shaking her head.

"A couple of days? A day? A couple of hours—what?" Midnight said gently.

"Maybe a day or two," Susan said, not sure how to answer the question.

Midnight nodded. "Do you remember the song Rick and I and Joe and Randy danced our first dance to at the wedding?"

"I remember it was beautiful, but I don't remember the title," Susan said, not sure what one had to do with the other.

"It was called 'Miss You in a Heartbeat,'" Midnight said. "And that's how it is with us. I love him that much. Joe loves Randy that much. That's how much I want you to love the man you marry."

"But Uncle Rick doesn't think that way, does he?" Susan said, having noted that Midnight kept saying "I," not "we."

Midnight sighed, sitting back in her chair. "Your uncle is thinking like an overprotective father right now. Not like a friend. He thinks that Warren is 'suitable.'" She said it as if it were a cuss word.

"But you don't."

"I'm judging him on a whole other criteria that has nothing to do with family name, prestige, money, or financial earnings projections. I'm judging him with my heart, and no, I don't think he's right for you. He's too much like—" She caught herself, realizing what she was about to say might be construed as an insult.

"Like my father," Susan finished for her, nodding. "Christian said the same thing the other day."

Midnight didn't reply; she just looked back at Susan as if to say, *See?* Midnight was surprised that Christian seemed to have insinuated himself so deeply in family business. Midnight considered Joe's family as much hers as Rick's family was now. Therefore Christian was, to her way of thinking, family too. But she also knew Christian liked to keep a cool distance from anything resembling emotion or affection. She'd figured out that much just from the few conversations they'd had. So she was surprised he'd come out championing something like Susan's poor choice of a mate. She pondered his involvement, wondering remotely at its origin.

They talked a little more as they ate lunch. Midnight dropped Susan off, hoping she'd made some impression on the girl. She started back to her and Rick's house, and looking at her watch, she noticed it was already 1:30. "Shit," she muttered under her breath.

She walked into their bedroom and saw that he was asleep on their bed. He was wearing jeans, so she knew he'd gotten up. When she drew close she could smell his aftershave and see that he'd shaved, and more than likely showered as well.

Quietly, she took off her clothes and, climbing carefully onto the bed, leaned down to kiss his chest, her copper-blond hair falling to brush his stomach. She moved her lips to his neck, kissing along the way. She felt him stir under her lips, and when she looked up his eyes were on her.

"Nice lunch?" he asked softly.

"Informative," she replied, moving to kiss him before he could ask anything else.

She lay over him then, her mouth never leaving his. She slid her body seductively down his and heard him groan against her lips. She grinned as he grasped her waist, pulling her hard against him. Midnight could feel his excitement and thought fleetingly of her conversation with Susan as she tugged at the buttons of his jeans. *Yes*, she thought as he pulled his jeans off. *Sexual attraction is very important!* Her thoughts turned to her husband as he pulled her to him again, his body sliding into hers. This was definitely important.

****

Deborah Debenshire arrived in San Diego three days later. Christian ended up being the one to pick her up from the airport. Rick had been busy with a case, Midnight had a council meeting, and Joe had nightmare for a desk when he returned from being off for three days. Christian had volunteered when he heard Midnight on the phone with Rick. Rick had called to see if Midnight could make it, and when she told him she couldn't, it became obvious to Christian that Rick was complaining about it. "I'll do it," he said from his place at her computer.

Midnight looked up, surprised, but then nodded gratefully. When she hung up she looked over at him. "Thanks a lot. I could see that one turning into a big fight. I originally told him I could pick her up, but this meeting got scheduled at the last minute."

"Don't worry about it," Christian said dismissively.

Three hours later he stood at the end of the gangway to flight 782 from London, waiting for a woman that looked like the picture he'd seen of Susan's mother. He was able to recognize her easily; she was one of the best-looking women getting off the plane, and she looked like she'd just left the beauty parlor rather than having just gotten through with a grueling twelve-hour flight.

"Deborah," Christian said, stepping forward as she approached.

She looked up at him, surprise clear in her deep blue eyes. "Yes?" she replied, her accent even more sophisticated than her daughter's.

"I'm Blue. I was asked by your sister-in-law to pick you up."

"Alright then," Deborah said, inclining her head.

Christian gestured for her to proceed him. They secured her luggage, which Christian easily carried outside. Once in the car, he remained silent, not sure what he should say to this woman. She reminded him of women like Geneva, who had it all, but he also knew she was divorcing her husband of many years because she wasn't happy. It was an interesting combination.

"So, you're Joseph's cousin," Deborah said politely.

Christian nodded. "Yeah."

"And the young man my father... helped," she said, her voice faltering at the end.

Christian's lips twisted in a sardonic grin. "I'm the guy he got out of jail, yeah." His accent was thick, as if he were trying to emphasize the differences between them.

"I didn't want to put it that way," Deborah said mildly.

"Why? Everybody that should know, does," Christian said, shrugging nonchalantly.

"Some people might be sensitive about having been under arrest…"

"I'm not—I'm glad I did it," Christian said, practically sneering, his light blue eyes focused on the road ahead.

Deborah was silent for a minute. She knew what Christian had done, not from her father but from other people in London society. One in particular.

"I have something for you, by the by," she said, her voice more upbeat now.

He raised one black eyebrow at her. "And what would that be?"

Deborah widened her eyes at him even as she began to grin. "Certainly not that," she said, far from offended. "It's a check."

"From who?" he replied, not understanding.

"From my father. It seems that he received the title for your Jaguar, and since he knew you couldn't use the car here, he sold it and has sent you the proceeds."

"I sent him the title," Christian said evenly.

"Well, he guessed that much, but he wasn't planning to charge you anything."

"He helped me out—I figured that merited payment." Christian was loath to accept any sort of charity.

"Yes, well, he figured he was doing family business. He is the Sinclairs' family lawyer, and you are a Sinclair." Now it was Deborah raising an eyebrow at him.

"No, I'm not," Christian said, hiding his amazement in his sour tone. He couldn't believe this cultured, groomed-to-the-teeth woman thought him a Sinclair too.

"I'm sorry," Deborah said sincerely. "But you are. You are very definitely Christian Jeremy Sinclair's son, and that makes you a Sinclair, regardless of what you're calling yourself."

Christian looked sharply over at the woman, trying to detect any sort of put down, but he couldn't see one.

"Speaking of that set," Deborah said, her tone changing again. "I spoke with Geneva Glasstone recently…" She trailed off as she glanced over to see his reaction.

The look on his face didn't change, but his eyes widened ever so slightly at the mention of the name.

"Yeah?" he said, his voice not belying his surprise.

"Yes, and she had nothing but good things to say about you, most of which I can't repeat in polite company."

Christian's grin was rakish as he shook his head. Leave it to Geneva to talk trash to society women.

"But what I'm wondering," Deborah said curiously, "is whether what she said about Sarah Sinclair and you is true."

Christian glanced at her, his eyes definitely reflecting surprise. He hadn't expected Geneva to say anything to anyone about that. He looked down, his lips curling in derision, but he nodded in answer to her question.

"Good lord. She was always the supreme princess of fidelity," Deborah said disdainfully.

"She wasn't that night," Christian said, his tone low and derogatory.

Deborah looked over at him. As he glanced at her, their eyes met and they both smiled.

"That's like sleeping with your stepmother, you know," she said lightly.

"She's nothin' to me. 'Cept *his* wife."

Deborah looked back at him, her deep blue eyes narrowing just slightly. "That's why you did it, wasn't it?"

"Damn straight," he replied, no apology in his voice.

"Do you always use women like that?" Deborah asked, her tone devoid of judgment.

"She wasn't *feelin'* used at the time," Christian countered confidently, his voice taking on a lurid timbre.

Deborah heard it, and felt herself respond to the sheer sexuality of the statement. She wasn't used to such an open discussion about sex. She knew she'd led a pretty sheltered existence as Wilson Endicott's wife, but this was a new level for her and she was enjoying it.

"What was she feeling?" Deborah surprised herself by asking, her voice just as lurid.

Christian looked over at her, his grin lopsided. "Everythin' but used."

"And what did you gain from the encounter?" Deborah asked a little breathlessly.

"Hearing his wife call out my name when I fucked her." He sounded almost angry now, carnal.

20

Deborah looked back at him, not understanding what he meant.

"My given name's Christian," he said, his voice softening ever so slightly.

"The same as your father's…"

"Yeah, but she was with me, not him."

Deborah nodded, understanding him now. "And that made all the difference."

Christian nodded. They continued the ride in silence.

When they arrived at the police department, Christian escorted Deborah to Midnight's office and went back to work, this time on the computer outside Midnight's room. Midnight and Deborah hugged, and then Deborah sat down in the chair across from the desk.

"So how's it going?" Midnight asked, referring to Deborah's divorce.

Deborah shrugged. "As well as can be expected. Wilson's not exactly one to fight about anything. Hell, I don't even think the divorce is bothering him."

Midnight looked doubtful, but nodded, knowing what Deborah meant.

"I think the only thing that bothers him is having to split up the assets," Deborah said, almost joking.

"Deborah!" Midnight said, laughing at her sister-in-law's cavalier attitude.

"What do you expect, Midnight?" Deborah smiled wide. "I haven't had the great marriage you and my brother have. Mine's been kind of like a job I hate for twenty-two years."

Midnight looked chagrined. "That bad, huh?"

"I think you know that," Deborah said insightfully. "You never liked Wilson, did you?"

Midnight looked embarrassed for a fraction of a second, but then shook her head. "I never understood what you saw in him. But I always figured I was comparing him to someone as incredible-looking as your brother, and that I wasn't being fair."

"You were being fair, but I think *incredible* would describe the young man sitting in your outer office right now."

"Blue?" Midnight said, her catlike eyes sparkling with excitement. "Yes, he is eye-catching, isn't he?"

"Drop-dead handsome is more like it. And the way he talks…" She trailed off as she looked heavenward.

"Sounds like he's got it on all the time, huh?" Midnight said conspiratorially.

"Good Lord, yes," Deborah said, her voice lowering the same way. Both women laughed.

"I always thought Joe was the gorgeous one in the family, but I'd have to say that Blue blows Joe away," Deborah said, shaking her head in disbelief.

"Hey, watch it," Midnight said, jokingly threatening. "That's my best friend you're talking about."

"Yes, and his cousin…" Deborah sounded surprised at that.

"Joe likes the kid," Midnight said. "I do too. He's pretty cool once you get past the ice-cold facade he keeps up."

"Yes, I noticed that," Deborah acquiesced.

Midnight grinned. "Hard to miss."

"So how is my daughter? Have you met this young man she's engaged to?"

Midnight rolled her eyes. "Oh yeah."

Deborah gave her sister-in-law a probing look. "What? You don't like him?"

"He reminds me of Wilson."

"But I thought he was American?"

"He is, but that doesn't seem to make any difference. He looks English, and he's about as dull as they come."

"And Susan fancies herself in love with him?"

"Well, I think her confidence in that may be waning..." Midnight trailed off as she thought about the conversation with Susan a few days before.

"Why do you say that?" Deborah asked.

"Her and I had lunch a few days ago, and she was asking a lot of questions that made me think she wasn't as sure about her engagement as she was before."

"What kinds of questions?" Deborah asked, curious what had changed her daughter's usually unchangeable mind.

"Questions about sexual attraction, and how important it was in a marriage." Midnight knew that was going to surprise Deborah.

She was right.

Deborah's eyes widened. "Really?"

"Yeah. I guess Warren's not exactly the best in the sex department," Midnight said disparagingly.

"Not another one of those…"

"Well, she wanted to know how important I thought sexual attraction was in a marriage," Midnight said judiciously, not sure how Deborah would react to what she'd told Susan. "I told her that in my marriage it was very important, because I was so attracted to her uncle. I… uh…"

"What?" Deborah asked. Midnight Chevalier-Debenshire was not given to caution when it came to saying what she thought.

"I kind of told her that I thought she should go out and test the water, so to speak… ya know?" Midnight looked a little solicitous at that point.

Deborah grinned at her sister-in-law. "Trust you to give it to my daughter straight," she said, with no anger in her voice. "That's probably what she needed to hear. She's so careful, you know. I guess she gets that from me. Always willing to do what other people want her to. It's a bad habit to fall into."

"Yeah, I told her that I thought she needed to know for sure before she married the guy that he was the one. I also told her that I wanted her to have a marriage like mine, or like Joe's, and she agreed wholeheartedly with that." Midnight shrugged, indicating that she didn't know if that meant Susan would change her mind or not.

"Well, I guess I'll meet the young man this afternoon," Deborah said.

That afternoon Christian drove up to the school, stopping where he usually picked Susan up. As he and Deborah waited, the radio was on and Christian sang along with some of the words. Deborah glanced over at him, surprised that he had such a nice voice.

24

Susan walked up then, hand in hand with Warren. Deborah looked at him, and then glanced back over at Christian. Christian rolled his eyes, shaking his head and looking out the window the opposite way. Deborah sighed and got out of the car.

Susan hugged her mother enthusiastically and then turned to Warren. "Mother, this is Warren Haley. Warren, my mother."

Deborah extended her hand to the young man, noting that Warren did indeed look a lot like Wilson. He would be considered nice-looking, but he was highly average, especially compared to men like Joe and Christian.

"It's nice to meet you," Warren said politely.

"You too," Deborah said, glancing at her daughter. She saw that Susan was looking over at Christian, who had turned his head to watch the meeting.

"I would like an opportunity to take you and your daughter to dinner, if you have time while you're here," Warren said, and Deborah nodded politely, thinking what a droll time that would be.

"Yes, I think that would be a lovely idea," she said, sounding very much like the polished aristocrat.

Warren nodded, then leaned over to kiss Susan on the cheek chastely.

Once they were in the car, Christian drove away almost immediately, not saying anything. Susan and her mother talked about what was going on at home, all the latest gossip. They both avoided mentioning the divorce. Eventually Susan couldn't resist asking the question that had been going around in her mind.

"What do you think of Warren, Mother?" she asked, her voice

almost begging her mother to say she liked him.

Deborah was silent for a long moment, glancing over at Christian, who grinned as he pointedly looked out the driver's window.

"He seems very nice, dear," she said finally.

"Nice?" Susan's tone indicated that she'd hoped for more of a description.

After a long moment, Christian couldn't contain his laughter. "I think you should quit while you're ahead."

"Shut up, you," Susan said, her voice taking on an edge.

"Susan!" Deborah exclaimed, surprised to hear her daughter so quick to react.

"I'm sorry, Mother, but you just have no idea what a hateful person he is." Susan narrowed her eyes at him as he continued to laugh softly.

Christian grinned. "No, I'm honest. You're just not used to that." It was clear her words didn't bother him one bit.

"You're contemptible and coarse," Susan said. "Perhaps you just don't know what that means."

"I know it means I'm getting under your skin, and it pisses you off all to hell," Christian replied coolly.

"I wish you'd just drop dead," Susan said, her anger almost making her sputter.

"I will, eventually," Christian said, his grin sardonic.

Deborah watched the exchange in shock. She'd never seen her daughter so reactive to another person before.

The following evening, Deborah and Susan drove over to Donovan's house to pick the children up. He'd had the day off and had given his sister a break with them. Deborah drove the black Jaguar, adapting easily to the American way of driving. She glanced over at her daughter. "So why is it you haven't learned to drive yet?" she asked lightly.

Susan looked over at her mother, knowing that despite her tone, Deborah was displeased. "I just haven't really taken the time. Warren said he'd teach me, but…" She trailed off as Deborah began shaking her head.

"Susan, you have got to start doing things for yourself. Don't expect a man to do everything for you. That makes you dependent on them, and that makes you foolish." Deborah's voice had turned sharp during her tirade, and it was obvious she was talking about herself too.

"Mother…" Susan began softly.

"Susan, you don't understand how hard this world can be on a woman with no courage to stand on her own. And if you can't stand on your own, you'll be too afraid to leave when you want to."

"What if I never want to?"

Deborah looked at Susan for a long moment, her face indicating how shortsighted she thought her daughter was. "If you marry that young man, I guarantee that you will eventually."

"You don't know that," Susan said, shocked at her mother's directness.

Deborah sighed. "Susan, I was married to your father for twenty-two years. For the first five years, I thought we were just adjusting to each other. Then I stayed because of you girls. But two years ago, I decided that I couldn't keep on the way I was. I wanted more out of life—I wanted excitement, and love."

"You didn't love Father?" Susan asked, almost hurt.

"I thought I did. I thought that making the commitment to marry him and to have children with him meant that I loved him. I thought that I could make everything the way I wanted it. But I couldn't. I wanted more. I wanted something like what your uncle has in his marriage. That kind of love, that kind of heat. Do you understand?" Deborah gave her daughter a long, hard look, trying to discern if she did understand.

"I guess I do… but Mother, I do love Warren," Susan said, striving to sound convincing.

"Do you?" Deborah asked, her voice indicating her disbelief.

Susan sighed. "Yes."

When they got to Donovan's, Jeanie answered the door. She and Donovan had spent the afternoon with the children. Jeanie had enjoyed it thoroughly, but she was pretty sure Donovan would be relieved when they were gone. She knew that while Donovan loved his niece and nephew, their propensity toward mass destruction tended to test his patience. His well-ordered home looked a lot less so by the time Kat and JT left.

Deborah walked into the kitchen with Jeanie and Susan trailing her. Donovan was standing at his cutting board, chopping vegetables. When he saw Deborah he smiled, setting down his knife and walking over to hug her.

"You've grown up since I saw you last, young man," Deborah said.

"Well, it's been about ten years, Deb," Donovan said, looking down at her and smiling widely.

"Good Lord, has it really been that long?"

"And then some," Donovan said, laughing. Then he gestured to Jeanie, who was standing holding JT on her hip. "Deborah, this is Jeanie. Jeanie, this is Deborah, Rick's sister."

"It's nice to meet you," Jeanie said, smiling and extending her hand to Deborah.

"And you as well," Deborah said, smiling back as she took it.

Susan and Jeanie went into the living room with the children, leaving Deborah standing in the kitchen with Donovan.

"She's beautiful, Donovan," Deborah whispered confidentially.

Donovan grinned and nodded. "Yeah, she is."

"Have you two been together long?"

"Only a few months."

"So, do you always cook, or is this a special occasion?" Deborah asked slyly.

Jeanie walked into the kitchen then, having left JT and Kat with Susan. She reached over to grab a vegetable off the cutting board and went to sit on the low island. Donovan smiled at her.

"Jay can vouch for me—I cook a lot," he told Deborah.

Jeanie nodded. "Yes, he does."

Donovan grinned. "Scary, huh?"

"On the contrary, it's quite refreshing," Deborah said.

"He's a very good cook, too," Jeanie said.

"Is that so?" Deborah asked, looking to Donovan again.

Donovan reached over and picked up his knife. "If you have time, stay for dinner and I'll prove it."

"You're on," Deborah replied.

A half hour later, Deborah happily agreed that Donovan was a great cook. Afterward, they sat in the living room, with the children and Susan on the floor. Jeanie and Donovan took the couch with Deborah. Jeanie sat in the circle of Donovan's arms, leaning back against him. They talked for a while, catching up on things that had happened since Donovan had seen Deborah last. Before long it became apparent that the children were getting tired, so Susan and Deborah left to take them home.

In the car, Deborah glanced over at her daughter. "So why didn't you grab him when you had the chance?" she asked lightly.

"Mother," Susan said, rolling her eyes.

"Donovan turned into a very handsome man, Susan. Don't tell me you didn't notice."

"Donovan's Joe's family, almost like a relative."

"Well, he's not your family," Deborah said.

It was obvious to Susan that her mother was thinking Donovan would have been a better catch than Warren. She sighed to herself, not sure she'd ever do the right thing in her mother's eyes.

CHAPTER 2

Malik Sobroy sat in the dark sedan, thinking that if he waited long enough the cop would up his price. Malik had grown up on the streets, and knew that jerks like this guy were always hitting up people like him to do their dirty work. Malik figured he deserved to get paid good for it. He turned his head, his dreadlocks sticking out at crazy angles, his almost black eyes set in very dark skin narrowing slightly. "So you want it done or not?" he asked, his tone sneering.

"Yeah, I want it done, but I'm gettin' fucked on the price." Frank Devereaux sounded irritated. He was sweating and nervous as hell. It was one thing to think about ordering a hit on a person; doing it was a whole other ball game.

"That's the price, take it or leave it."

Devereaux narrowed his eyes at the young man, knowing he was getting ripped off but not willing to take the chance of approaching someone else to do this job. "Fine, half now, and half when it's done," he said, pulling out an envelope and handing it over. "You got the details? Who and where?"

"Yeah, man, I got 'em." Malik rolled his eyes, then pinned the cop with a look. "Jus' 'cause I'm black, don't mean I'm stupid too."

Devereaux grunted, not willing to get into a fight with the kid. "Fine then. I'll wait to hear the news, and you'll get the rest then."

"Right." Malik got out of the car and watched it drive away. He turned around, heading for the grocery store. His girlfriend would be happy as hell if he actually brought some food home for a change.

Christian dropped Susan off at school, and with Deborah in the car drove toward the office. She was going to use the car that day to do some shopping and just "goof off." On the way downtown he flipped through the radio stations, catching the very end of a song he liked.

"Shit," he uttered as he continued to change stations. He glanced apologetically over at Deborah. "Sorry," he said, chagrined at having cussed in front of her.

Deborah gave him a caustic look. "I grew up with my brother and Joseph, remember? I've heard much worse than that."

Christian gave her an appraising look, then shrugged. "You just look so proper, I guess I just figured…"

"Well, I'm not that proper," Deborah assured him.

Christian didn't look convinced. "You look pretty proper to me. 'Course, that may be because I'm so far from," he said, his tone holding no remorse at his lack of decorum.

"Well, I am still too proper for my own good," Deborah said, shaking her head.

Christian grinned. "You could stand a little loosening up, yeah."

Deborah raised an eyebrow at him. "And I'll bet you could teach me a thing or two about that, couldn't you?"

"Oh yeah." Christian nodded, looking amused at the thought.

They arrived at the department a little while later, and Christian got out, handing her the keys as she came around to the driver's side. "I get off at four thirty. Your daughter's got a lab tonight and her dear

32

fiancé will be escorting her home. If you're still in the mood to loosen up by then, we'll go have a few drinks."

Deborah grinned at him and nodded.

It was around 3:00 that afternoon when they heard the radio call. Midnight, Christian, and Jeanie were in her office discussing the new inventory program when Cassandra threw the door open.

"Midnight!" she said, almost frantic. "Listen!" She went over to the police radio. "They just picked up this call from East San Diego."

There was the usual traffic and then the call came again. "1199 officer down, East San Diego, Home and El Cajon Boulevard..." The voice trailed off, and then there was a clattering sound as the officer apparently dropped the mike, cutting off the transmission.

Everything happened at once, Midnight standing, as did Jeanie.

"I gotta go," Jeanie said, shaking her head. She looked very pale, already visibly shaking.

"Who was that?" Midnight asked, having not recognized the voice.

"It was Donovan," Jeanie said, heading for the door.

"Jeanie, wait!" Christian blocked her exit. "You can't drive, not like this. I'll take you. Ah, shit, I don't have the car today."

"Take mine," Midnight said, tossing him the keys. "I'll get ahold of Joe and have him get ahold of Randy."

Christian nodded. "Where would they take him?" he asked very calmly, even as his insides shuddered at the thoughts running through his head.

"Mercy—it's over off of 160." Midnight was already picking up her phone to locate Joe.

"Got it," he said, taking Jeanie gently by the arm. "Come on."

An hour and a half later, Midnight, Joe, and Randy joined Jeanie and Christian in the waiting room at the hospital. "Have they said anything yet?" Joe asked.

"He's in surgery," Christian said, pulling Joe aside. "They said he was shot, twice."

Joe looked surprised, his light blue eyes widening. Then he glanced over at his wife. He knew Randy was holding on to her control as tightly as possible. To her Donovan was like her son, and she was reacting like a mother would at hearing that her child was in surgery.

The doctor came out three hours later. The main members of FORS and a few other officers had joined the original group. Joe, Randy, and Jeanie stood when the man walked up.

"He's out of surgery," the doctor said, his tone very business-like. "He was a very lucky young man. He was shot in the left shoulder and in the upper-left side of his torso. The second bullet missed his heart by approximately a quarter of an inch."

"When can we see him?" Joe asked, holding tightly to Randy's hand, having felt her waver when the man said the last.

"In about two hours," the doctor replied. "A nurse will come get you."

"Thanks." Joe turned to look at Randy. "You okay?" he asked, knowing she wasn't.

Randy looked at him for a long moment, then nodded weakly.

Midnight came back a little while later; she'd been on the phone with the office, trying to find out what had happened. "How's he doin'?" she asked, looking down at her partner.

"They said he was lucky, that one of the bullets just missed his heart," Joe recited, feeling numb.

Midnight nodded, looking grim. "When can you guys see him?"

"They said two hours," Joe replied.

"Okay." Midnight nodded again. "I'm gonna head out to the site. I wanna talk around and find out what happened. Right now they're calling it an attempted carjacking."

Joe looked at her for a long moment, sickened at the thought. The idea that the car Donovan was so proud of may have caused this was too much to bear at that point.

Midnight left, and two hours later Joe, Randy, and Jeanie were able to go in to see Donovan. Joe told the nurse that Jeanie was a relative, to gain her access to his room.

Inside, Randy leaned heavily against Joe. Donovan lay in the hospital bed, his chest bare, with bandages covering the two wounds. He had an IV in his arm and monitors surrounding him as well.

Jeanie walked over to the bed and reached out a shaking hand to brush a lock of sandy-brown hair off his forehead. Donovan stirred, opening his eyes. He looked at her, then over at Randy and Joe, then closed his eyes slowly as if trying to gain strength. When he opened his eyes again, he looked at Jeanie, who had tears on her cheeks. His right hand moved to touch hers, even as he stared into her eyes. "Hey," he said quietly, his voice gravelly.

"Hey yourself, Sergeant," Jeanie said, her voice equally soft and colored with emotion.

He closed his eyes a moment later, and it was obvious he was asleep again. Randy and Joe had watched from the foot of the bed. They spent the next three hours waiting for word from Midnight on what had happened and watching Donovan sleep.

Midnight arrived back at the hospital and went directly to Donovan's room. The moment she stepped inside, Joe knew something was up. He walked over to her, his expression grave. "What's goin' on, Night? What'd you find out?"

"I don't know if I should tell you here," Midnight said, looking over at Randy, who was watching them from her place on Donovan's left.

"Just tell me. Randy'll hear it one way or the other," Joe said, knowing that his wife was listening and knowing from the look on Midnight's face she wasn't going to like what she was about to hear. He didn't know how right he was.

"Look," Midnight said hesitantly. "I talked to a lot of witnesses at the scene, and they all come up with the same thing." She hesitated again, noting that Jeanie was listening intently now too. Joe nodded, wanting her to continue. "Donovan was stopped at a light. Two black males pulled up behind him in a dark-colored older-model car. They got out and flanked Donovan's car. The one on the driver's side opened the door and dragged Donovan out of the car and shoved him down on his knees. He produced a gun and pointed it directly at Donovan's head." She paused as the impact of what she was saying hit

Joe. He closed his eyes, feeling sick. Midnight started to nod, knowing he understood what it meant. She looked over at Jeanie, who looked perplexed by the whole thing. "They were planning to kill him, Jeanie, to execute him, gangland style."

"What does that mean?" Randy asked in a choked voice, unable to fathom what was happening.

"It means," Joe said, moving to his wife's side, "that these guys weren't looking to jack his car. They were looking to kill him. It was a hit."

"We're getting close to them, and they know it," Midnight said, leaning against the wall, her expression drawn and angry.

"This has to do with the case?" Jeanie asked, clearly shocked.

Midnight nodded. "Donovan's quick reactions and luck were what saved his life," she said, looking at him as he slept. "I guess the kid with the gun hesitated, probably more for dramatics than anything, giving his target a chance to realize what was about to happen to him. That's when Donovan reacted. He said he fell back, going for his gun at the same moment. The kid fired the first time then, catching Donovan in the shoulder. Donovan cleared his holster and brought his gun up. The kid got scared and fired again, then ran like hell. Witnesses think Donovan got off three, maybe four shots, and they're pretty sure he winged one of them. I've already alerted all the local hospitals and clinics in case one of 'em shows up for treatment."

Randy had been staring at Midnight as she described the incident. The look on her face indicated that she couldn't believe what she was hearing. This was her baby brother, and these "kids" had tried to kill him in cold blood. All because of a case. Randy had to clamp down on the anger that flooded her veins. She wanted to scream at Midnight for putting her brother in that kind of danger. She wanted to scream at Joe for letting her. Eventually she had to get up and walk out of the room, knowing if she didn't she'd do what she wanted to so badly. Joe waited for a few minutes, understanding the rage Randy was feeling and knowing she needed to be alone to vent it.

Jeanie couldn't believe what she had heard either. She looked at Donovan, holding his hand gently and thinking that she could have been staring at a corpse at that moment. Joe left the room a few minutes later, and Midnight followed him, indicating she was going to check in with the office. Jeanie sat next to Donovan, watching him, trying to make sense of everything. She knew it was extremely bad that the people they were investigating had decided to try and take out a member of the team. She knew it could have just as easily been her, or Cassandra or Midnight. It scared her.

Christian had stayed with Jeanie at the hospital, making sure she was alright, until Joe and Randy arrived. Then he'd used the cell phone in Joe's Jaguar to get ahold of Deborah and let her know what was going on. He asked her to pick him up, and gave Joe Midnight's keys. When Deborah arrived at the hospital they still didn't know how Donovan was, but Christian felt the urgent need to get away. It was too much for him; he hated the idea of Randy's brother being shot, and he didn't know the nature of the shooting or if Donovan would pull through. He knew his cousin and Randy were in agony waiting to hear, and he couldn't handle it. Christian got into the driver's side of the car, glancing over at Deborah.

"I don't know about you," he said, depressed, "but I certainly need a drink right now."

He reached over and turned the radio up. They drove toward the bar in Pacific Beach that Christian now frequented because of Tara. He and Tara had spent a couple more nights together. She'd been just as easygoing, and he was glad of that. He hated clingy women.

When they arrived, he escorted Deborah inside. He sat down at the bar, ordered a double shot of tequila from Tara for himself, and asked Deborah what she wanted. She ordered a glass of Chivas Regal. They spent the next two hours drinking. By the time they drove home Deborah was feeling quite loosened up. The song "I Need a Lover," a remake by John Cougar Mellencamp, came on the radio. She listened to the words and watched as Christian sang them, looking like he meant every word. The lyrics talked about needing a lover that wouldn't drive him crazy.

Deborah grinned as the song ended. "That's what you want, isn't it?" she said, her tone not accusatory in the least.

He nodded. "Usually."

"See…" Deborah said, leaning her head back against the passenger seat and closing her eyes. "That's what I need right now. I feel so out of touch with reality lately. It's like I've come out of this coma to find out that the whole world has changed. I don't know how to do this single thing anymore."

Christian glanced over at her. "You'll get the hang of it." He knew she'd had too much to drink. He himself was actually feeling a pretty good buzz, and he knew he shouldn't really be driving. He took extra care not to drive too fast, or too erratically.

"I don't know… this sex thing," Deborah said, shaking her head. "I haven't had a whole lot of practice. You don't understand," she said hesitantly.

"How long were you married?" Christian asked, glancing at her again.

"Twenty-two years."

"And you didn't get in enough practice in all that time?" Christian asked cynically.

"Are you kidding?" Deborah raised an eyebrow at him, then nodded. "That's right, you never met Wilson. My husband was, shall we say, negligent in his husbandly duties. And when he did get around to it, it wasn't exactly earth-shaking."

"Okay..." Christian said slowly. "So you're a little out of practice—you'll pick it up again."

"That would indicate that I knew what I was doing in the first place," Deborah said caustically. "I only had one other lover before I married Wilson, and he was just as inexperienced as I was."

Christian made a face, indicating his distaste for ineptitude in this area. "Well, that's not altogether good, is it?" he said, his grin wry.

"Quite."

"So what did you do while you were married? I mean, you obviously never had an affair—what'd you do?"

"I shopped a lot," Deborah replied, sounding very matter of fact.

"Christ." Christian shook his head ruefully. "You got more willpower than I'd ever have had."

"I'm very proper, remember?" Deborah replied, making the word sound derogatory.

"Well, I'd say you were too proper," Christian said as they pulled up to Joe and Randy's house. He got out of the car and went to open Deborah's door for her.

Once inside the house, they noted that Joe and Randy weren't home yet. The place was silent.

"So, where is it you stay?" Deborah asked as he headed toward the back of the house.

Christian turned around, looking at her for a long moment. Then he canted his head in the direction he'd been heading. "Out back there." He shrugged. "I couldn't handle being so close to people all the time."

"Can I see it?" Deborah asked, loath to be alone at that point.

Christian shrugged again. "I guess. There ain't much to see though." He led her out to the carriage house, careful to make sure the alarm was armed for the main house first.

In his room, he and Deborah ended up sitting on the bed talking for another hour. They talked about her marriage, and why she'd pursued Wilson in the first place and how the marriage had been doomed from the start. She told him she'd gone on because of the girls, never really realizing what she was missing. Then she told him about how when Midnight and Rick had visited a couple of years before looking so blissfully in love with each other, she'd finally realized she was wasting her life on a man she didn't love. She told Christian how she wanted to meet a man that excited her senses, her mind, and her body. He said he thought that was a reasonable expectation in someone you were married to.

Deborah grimaced. "Yes, well, when you don't know any better…"

"I think you did. I think you just avoided seeing it for a long time," Christian said wisely, drinking from the glass of Jack Daniels he'd poured himself. Deborah was drinking as well, having tried the whiskey for the first time.

"Maybe. I don't know," she said, shrugging. "I do know that I will not settle for just anything anymore. I just worry that..." She trailed off, as if she'd decided not to finish the sentence.

"Worry that what?" Christian asked, sitting up and looking down at her.

Deborah looked up at him, staring directly into his eyes. "I just don't have any real basis for comparison, that's all."

"Is that what you're looking for?" he asked, his tone lowering significantly.

"What?" Deborah asked, her voice a whisper, her dark blue eyes not looking away from his.

"A basis for comparison." Christian moved a couple of inches closer to her and heard her breathing deepen.

"I..." Deborah began, but his lips on hers stopped her. Whatever she'd been about to say went right out of her head the second his hands closed around her waist, pulling her body up to his. The kiss was intense and alcohol-driven. Deborah felt her whole body begin to shake, and she knew that what they were doing was crazy, but she couldn't pull away. Before she knew what was happening they were lying on the bed, and things moved very quickly from there. She couldn't think, she couldn't stop, and she couldn't control the actions of her own body. In minutes she wanted him more than she'd ever wanted anything. When his body entered hers, she cried out, grasping at his shoulders as he moved above her. She found herself saying and doing things she'd never done, all the while following his lead. Christian pushed her to heights above and beyond anything she'd ever achieved in twenty-two years of marriage, or even imagined.

Afterward Deborah lay over him, trying desperately to catch her breath. When she was able to, she moved to her side, looking at him. His light blue eyes watched her, a knowing look on his face that was just short of smug.

"I'm not sure what to say at a time like this," she said quietly.

Christian laughed softly. "You don't have to *say* anythin'," he replied, sounding very English and very young at the same time.

"This was hardly what I expected to be doing this evening," Deborah said, feeling the need to excuse her behavior in some way.

"So, shit happens," Christian said humorously, still watching her.

"Ah, yes, except you're young enough to be my son," Deborah said caustically.

"So?" Christian replied drily. "I'm not—that's what counts."

She shook her head. "Yes, but—"

"Deborah," Christian said, placing his hand on her cheek. "We did it, it was good. Let it go at that." His look was entreating. "You women always overthink everything. Can't you just get off on the feeling, on the actual sex? It doesn't have to mean a damn thing to be good."

Deborah looked at him for a long moment. He was telling her to lighten up, and she knew he was letting her off the hook in a way too. Finally she nodded, closing her eyes. "You're right. It was certainly a hell of a way to start out my new life."

"There you go," Christian said, grinning.

They both slept for a little while after that, and eventually Deborah left, after kissing him deeply and uttering a simple word of thanks. They both knew that nothing would be said about this night—it wasn't for anyone to know. It was between them. They didn't discuss it, but it was understood.

Jeanie was asleep in the chair next to Donovan's bed when he woke the second time. Joe had long since dragged Randy home, telling Jeanie they'd come back in the morning. Donovan's head moved around as he came back to consciousness, then his hand clenched, squeezing Jeanie's, which he still held. She woke immediately and watched as he grimaced a couple of times then slowly opened his eyes. "Hi," she said softly, moving to kiss his cheek.

Donovan smiled slightly and shifted around a little, as if trying to get comfortable. He winced when he jarred his shoulder.

"Are you hurting a lot?" Jeanie asked.

"Some," he said, sounding out of breath.

"Do you want me to get a nurse?"

"No, I'm okay," Donovan said, his voice a little stronger. Then his look deepened as he noted the expression in her eyes. "Jay, I'm okay, *really*." They both knew he was talking about more than the pain he was in at that moment.

"Then you do remember what happened?" Jeanie asked, her voice pained.

Donovan nodded slowly, closing his eyes as he thought about the attack. "They were out for a hit," he said gravely.

Jeanie nodded. "That's what Midnight thinks. She said you shot one of them though—do you think you might have?"

Donovan thought about it for a minute, then nodded. "I might have. I think I got off about four shots... I'm not sure."

Jeanie nodded. "Witnesses thought either three or four shots. But Donovan, how? I mean, you were shot in the left shoulder. You're left-handed—how did you manage to shoot?"

Donovan looked at her for a long moment, grinning at the fact that she knew him well enough to remember he was left-handed. "When I saw them get out of the car I reached back and cocked my gun. I don't know exactly why, but I just knew they were out for no good." He shook his head then, looking tired.

Jeanie reached out, touching his cheek. He closed his eyes in response. "You rest, babe," she said.

Donovan nodded, pulling her hand up close to his face, kissing her fingers gently. He slept.

That night Joe and Randy were in bed together. Randy lay with her head against his chest as he stroked her hair.

"You okay?" Joe asked, knowing what he was asking.

"Not really," Randy said tonelessly.

"Go ahead, Randy. I know you have stuff you want to say—just go ahead." Joe's voice held no anger. He wanted to know what was going on inside her head.

"I just want to know how far you two are going to let this go," Randy said angrily.

"Let it go?" Joe repeated, surprised at her choice of words.

"Yeah. I mean, why does every fight Midnight has have an effect on me and my own? Why can't she just let it go?"

"Randy," Joe said disbelievingly. "You can't think that she knew these guys would try to kill Donovan? That she doesn't care that a member of her team just got shot because of a case she's got him working on. Randy, she cares about Donovan just as much—"

"Just as much as the rest of her staff, her team," Randy replied, cutting him off angrily.

"Just as much as *I do*," Joe continued. "Jesus Christ, Randy, you know Midnight thinks a lot of Donovan. Hell, he's practically her little brother all over again."

"Yeah, and she got *him* killed," Randy retorted.

Joe sat up, disengaging himself from her. He looked down at her, stunned, as if he didn't know her. He started to shake his head. "Don't ever say that again," he said, his light blue eyes burning with anger. "You know damn good and well that's not true, and you know just as well that she has to do what she's doing."

Randy sat up, surprised by the vehemence in his voice and knowing she'd gone too far, saying what she'd said about Midnight's brother. But she was angry and upset at the thought of Donovan being executed in the middle of the street for nothing more than his job. It was her anger that made her speak now.

"No, I don't know that she has to do what she's doing. So some cops are making some money—who cares, they're harmless. Who's losing, Joe, the dirtbags you're taking the money off of? Who the fuck cares?"

"Who cares? Randy, you don't fucking get it, do you?" Joe shook his head. "Those cops—those harmless cops—just ordered a hit on

46

your little brother. You think they did that on a whim? You think Midnight couldn't be next, or me? They are doing a lot more than stealing money, Randy, and they don't care about killing another cop to keep on doing it. And you don't think Midnight has to stop them? Didn't you learn anything from last time? The shit with Dickerson, didn't you see what could happen when people thought the law didn't apply to them? The law does apply, and it's Midnight's and my and Donovan's job to enforce that. Donovan knew what was involved when he took this job."

"Okay," Randy said, not willing to be placated so easily. "So what happens when it is you they come after next? What happens if they come after your children, Joe? Are you going to be so sure…" She trailed off as she saw the stricken look on his face. She knew she had just caused him a lot of pain. In her attempt to alleviate her own fears about her brother, she'd dealt him a new fear. She realized it too late, and reached out to touch him, trying to pull back the words she'd just said. "Joe…"

He shook his head, moving to lie back down, the look on his face not changing. "Randy… God," he said, blowing his breath out in an almost painful sigh. "I can't think about all that. I can't think how everything I do can affect everything else…" He trailed off as the possibilities hit him. He shook his head miserably.

Randy lay down next to him, reaching up to pull him into an embrace, clinging to him. "I'm sorry, Joe. I'm sorry. That wasn't fair. I just… I was so afraid for Donovan, and then hearing that he could have been murdered… I wanted to scream and yell. And now we talk about it, and you get defensive of Midnight and I guess I just reacted to that. I'm sorry, I am. Shit," she said then, knowing there was no way to stop the hurt she'd caused.

47

"Hey," Joe said, hugging her tight. "I know you're upset about Donovan, and I knew you were mad at the hospital. I knew the can of worms I was opening when I asked if you were okay. I guess I just didn't think it would get so nasty."

"That's me—that's my fault, Joe," Randy said, shaking her head. "I just get crazy when it comes to Donovan. He's like my own son, you know. I've just always worried about him, and taken care of him. And now I have no control over anything that happens, and him being shot is the polarization of all my fears, you know…"

"Yeah, babe, I know," Joe said. "But he's okay—he's fine. His training took over, just like it should have. That's what got him out of that."

"Yeah, and I guess I have you to thank for that good training, huh?" Randy sounded chagrined.

Joe didn't answer, he just nuzzled her hair, kissing her on the temple. "Everything'll be fine."

They didn't talk anymore, but Randy knew he was thinking about what she had said. And she knew there was no way to shut off the fears that she'd started in him.

The next morning Joe told Susan what had happened to Donovan. He also told her that he didn't want her taking the children out of the house without either himself or Christian with her. He also didn't want her going anywhere without one of them with her for the time being. Susan nodded seriously, listening to every word Joe said.

Christian sat at the table listening as well, looking equally serious. It surprised him that he was actually angry that someone had tried to kill Donovan in cold blood. He thought Donovan was a pretty good guy for the most part, even if they didn't exactly get along all the time. Most of the time because Christian couldn't resist baiting him about Jeanie.

****

The next couple of weeks were tense. The two young men who had attempted to kill Donovan didn't turn up. Midnight, predictably, dug her heels in, and worked on the case almost fanatically. Rick noticed she was exhausted almost all of the time, but she kept working. He tried to convince her to slow down, but he knew his wife was feeling the need to stop the men that attempted to kill Donovan.

One day, two weeks after Donovan was shot, Midnight was working in her office. Christian was sitting at her table looking over sheets of printouts. Midnight stood from her desk, stretching. Christian glanced up and noticed she looked tired. As he watched her she closed her eyes for a moment, then started to fall. Christian jumped up and leapt across the desk, catching her. She'd passed out cold.

"Midnight!" he exclaimed, looking down at her face. He touched her cheek—it was cold. He looked around, knowing he needed to do something. She stirred then, and he called her name again.

Midnight opened her eyes, looking confused. "What happened?" she asked, looking up at him.

"You passed out, Chief," he said. "I'm gonna get you to a doctor." He stood, picking her up easily.

"I'm fine," Midnight said, looking anything but; she was pale.

"Yeah, and when the doctor tells me that I'll let you go home," Christian said, moving toward the door. He held Midnight in his arms, and she surprisingly gave up, leaning her head against his shoulder. In truth she still felt pretty weak, and didn't have the strength to fight him. She guessed correctly that arguing with Christian Collins about her well-being was as hopeless as arguing with his cousin. In the outer office, Cassandra stared openmouthed as Christian came out of Midnight's office carrying the chief.

"Cassandra," Christian said, stopping at her desk. "I'm taking the chief to the doctor. Could you please get ahold of her husband and let him know where she'll be?"

"Okay," Cassandra said, nodding numbly.

Two hours later, Rick Debenshire arrived at Mercy Hospital and walked into his wife's room.

"What happened?" he asked, looking at Midnight, who sat on the bed looking perfectly fine, and then glancing at Christian, who was leaning against the wall next to the bed.

"I passed out, no big deal," Midnight said, shrugging.

"No big deal?" Rick shook his head at his wife. "And why did you pass out?"

"Who knows." Midnight rolled her eyes. "You said yourself I've been overdoing it lately—maybe I'm just overly tired."

"Yeah, maybe," Rick said, not looking convinced. "What did the doctor say?"

Midnight shrugged again. "So far all the tests they've run have come back normal."

"Uh-huh," Rick said, nodding. "I'll be back." He turned and walked out the door.

Midnight sat staring at the door, looking perplexed. She glanced over at Christian, who raised a jet black eyebrow and shook his head. Rick came back a few minutes later. This time he walked over to the bed and looked down at his wife. His eyes searched hers, and she stared back at him, trying to figure out what he was searching for.

"What?" she said, knowing him well enough to know something was wrong.

Rick just shook his head, glancing over at Christian. "Thanks for bringing her here," he said to the younger man.

"No problem."

Midnight's doctor walked in then, and Rick turned to him, his face drawn. Midnight looked from her husband to the doctor and noticed the expression both men wore was the same. It bothered her.

"Okay," she said, sighing. "What the hell's goin' on?"

"Midnight," the doctor said, his tone cautionary. When he didn't continue she got impatient.

"What is it already? You said all the tests were normal, for God's sake—now what's happened?"

"Night," Rick said, turning to her and taking her hand.

"Shit, don't do that," she said, staring up into his eyes as the doctor started to talk again.

"Midnight, it seems as though you've somehow beaten the odds. You're pregnant."

All the color left Midnight's face as she stared openmouthed at her husband then turned to look at the doctor. Christian watched from his place in the corner, wondering why everyone appeared so grave at this news.

"But... I... you..." Midnight stammered. "You said it wasn't possible, after last time..." Midnight's voice trailed off as she shook her head. She couldn't believe what she'd just heard.

"Well, we thought that due to the damage to your uterus and the subsequent scarring you would be incapable of becoming pregnant again. Obviously, that was incorrect. There may have been less scarring than we expected, or your uterus may have substantiated itself more from the time of the miscarriage. It's hard to say." The doctor sounded very clinical and business-like even when he segued into the next part of his diagnosis. "Now the important thing here is that we caught it early. It will cause a lot fewer complications this time. We can even take care of it tomorrow morning, since we'd like to keep you overnight for observation in any case. I'd like to go ahead and schedule the procedure first thing, and a DNC. I would suggest that you consider a hysterectomy at this point. It would keep this from happening again. Considering the complications you are most likely in for in the near future, that may alleviate that problem as well."

Rick had watched the doctor for a few moments when he began to speak, but then his attention was drawn back to his wife. He could see her listening to the doctor, but he could also see her mind working, and he didn't like the look on her face.

When the doctor concluded his diagnosis it took Midnight a long moment to realize he'd stopped talking. She'd been thinking about the fact that against all odds she was pregnant again. Her mind had ceased to listen at that moment. Rick's hand on her cheek made her turn toward him, his deep blue eyes searching hers as she gazed up at him. What he saw in her eyes terrified him instantly.

Rick looked at the doctor. "Look, give us a minute, okay?"

The man nodded, understanding the intense people he was dealing with. Christian wondered if they had forgotten he was in the room; in truth, they both had.

Rick looked at Midnight for a long moment, then started to shake his head. "No, Midnight," he said, deadly serious. "I can see what you're thinking, and just stop right now."

"Wait—" Midnight started to say, but Rick made a cutting gesture with his hand as he cut her off verbally as well.

"No!" he yelled, as if with the force of his voice alone he could stop her from the dangerous course of her thoughts. "This is not up for discussion, Midnight. You are not having this baby, and I'll be damned if I'll let you even considered it for a fraction of a second longer." His eyes were hard, his face a mask of determined anger.

Midnight's eyes narrowed then, and Christian would have sworn he could literally feel the electricity in the room.

"This isn't your decision," Midnight said softly, but with a timbre that Christian already recognized as her cold determination.

"It isn't a fucking decision, Midnight!" Rick railed, his fear for her well-being making his voice icy. "It happened, and now it's going to be taken care of, and it won't happen again. One way or the other."

"Like you'll never sleep with me again, right?"

"No, like I'll take care of it from my end if that's what it takes," he said, the look on his face serious.

Midnight didn't say anything. She just stared back at him, her eyes giving nothing away. A nurse walked into the room then, glancing from Rick to Midnight.

"Mrs. Debenshire, I understand we need to schedule a procedure…" She trailed off as she noted the look on Midnight's face. "I can come back."

"Yes, why don't you do that," Midnight said, her tone anything but accommodating.

"No," Rick said, stopping the nurse. "Just schedule it for the morning." The nurse nodded, looking unsure but writing down the information anyway. She left the room, and Rick turned back to Midnight, who was looking up at him, her face calm, almost serene. It alarmed Rick immediately.

"*You are doing this*, Midnight," he said.

Midnight raised an eyebrow at him, her expression confident. "No," she said simply.

With that she stood up, walking past her husband and out of the room. Christian watched, both jet black eyebrows raised in stunned silence. Rick glanced over then, as if seeing Christian for the first time, his mouth still hanging open in appalled fury. He closed his eyes for a minute, then, shaking his head and making a disgusted sound in the back of his throat, went after his wife. Christian left the room a little while later, having seen firsthand what it would be like to be married to a spitfire like Midnight Chevalier. He didn't relish the thought.

Rick was feeling the same when he caught up to Midnight out in the parking lot. She'd gotten outside and realized her car was still back at the department.

"Need a ride?" Rick asked sarcastically.

"Funny," Midnight said, her face indicating anything but humor.

On the drive home, Rick was quiet. He rested his elbow on his window, his index finger rubbing across his lips, something he did when he was agitated. Midnight knew he was thinking about what to say. The radio was on, but it was down low. Midnight tuned in to the song that was playing and looked sharply over at him. It was their song, and she wondered how he'd managed that.

As if tuning in to her thoughts, Rick glanced over at her and then at the radio. Reaching over, he turned it up. The verse that they both loved came up and Rick sang the words, looking at her.

He touched the wedding ring she wore and glanced at her. "Doesn't this mean anything to you?" he asked, his voice desolate.

"It means everything to me, Rick," Midnight said, taking his hand in hers. "That's why I want this baby." Her look was entreating, begging him to understand.

Rick stared at her for a long moment, then shook his head. "No, Midnight, you're not doing this. We're not taking this chance."

"Rick—" she began, hoping to appeal to him.

He cut her off. "No! Damn it, Midnight, no!"

Midnight was silent then, and Rick knew her well enough to know that was far from acquiescence for her. Usually it meant just the opposite. He found out later that night how right he was.

They argued for hours, going from fury to tears to silence. Finally, late that evening, Midnight simply shrugged and said, "I guess we have an impasse."

"And…" Rick said, knowing her well.

"And I'm keeping this baby, and you're just going to deal with it."

"I will drag you down to that hospital kicking and screaming if I have to," he said, not for the first time that evening.

"Yeah, but I have to sign the papers," Midnight said calmly, her expression confident. "And I ain't signing anything."

Rick stared back at her, feeling as impotent as was physically possible at that moment. His deep blue eyes blazed at her, his hands curling into fists of reined-in fury. Again, Midnight took the opportunity to walk away. She went into their room. Rick found her asleep in their bed an hour later. He had made a point of drinking a number of shots of tequila before attempting to go into the bedroom. He'd needed it to calm down. As he crawled into bed next to her, he felt her tense. Heedless of her tension, he slid his arms around her, pulling her back against him.

"I love you, Midnight. Please don't do this," he whispered against her temple.

"I have to," Midnight whispered back.

Rick fell asleep with a knot in the pit of his stomach and a fair-sized lump in his throat.

****

While Donovan was in the hospital, Jeanie got word that her application for police officer training had been approved. She started at the academy the day Donovan was released. She arrived at his house at six o'clock that evening. Donovan was sitting up in his bed, and his sister was buzzing about trying to make sure he was comfortable. Basically, she was driving him crazy. When Jeanie walked into the bedroom his smile was brilliant, and she couldn't resist sitting next to him, kissing him softly on the lips.

The weeks Donovan had been in the hospital had been very difficult. Jeanie had been terrified when he was shot, and it had brought reality to her in a flash. Suddenly she'd been able to see graphically what could happen to someone she cared about, or even to her. One minute you were fine, the next you could be gone. It made everything very real. Donovan had been very quiet while in the hospital, indicating to Jeanie that he was dealing with the same realities.

Now, sitting next to him, Jeanie remembered some of the things they had said at the academy that day. The instructors had talked about how being a police officer was more than a regular eight-hour-a-day job. "You are a cop twenty-four seven," Sergeant Briggs told the trainees. "There is no real time off. You are on the job all the time."

As she looked at Donovan she thought of it again.

"What?" Donovan asked, his eyes searching hers. He'd noticed her distance from him over the last few weeks, and wondered what was going on inside her head.

"Nothing," she said. "I'm going to go change. I'll be right back." She stood and headed for his bathroom.

Donovan lay back, resting his head on the headboard and closing his eyes. He heard the door to his bedroom open and assumed it was Randy coming back in. That was why he was surprised when he opened his eyes. His mouth literally dropped open, and he couldn't think of a thing to say. Serena stood next to the bed, looking down at him. She looked like she had seven years before. Her long red hair was pulled back from her face, her green eyes shining at him.

"Hi. Randy let me in," she said softly. It was obvious she was unsure what to say as well.

"Hi," Donovan said, nodding and struggling to regain his senses.

Serena looked back at the man that had been her fiancé years before. Her heart was pounding very hard in her chest. She couldn't believe he was actually more handsome now than he had been before. His teal eyes were emphasized by his tan, and by his sandy-brown hair worn longer than it had been. His shirt was unbuttoned, and she could see that his chest was much more defined. He was incredible, and she was stunned.

"What're you doing here?" Donovan asked, regaining his composure faster than she did.

"I... I was visiting my family, and I planned on looking you up anyway, then I heard about the shooting. Are you really okay?" she asked, concern coloring her voice as she sat down on the bed.

"So they tell me," Donovan said, looking only partially convinced.

"You were shot twice?" Serena asked, her eyes taking in the bandage on his upper torso.

"Yeah." Donovan moved carefully to open his shirt, showing her the bandage on his shoulder. Serena grimaced, shaking her head.

"Nice business you got yourself into," she said deprecatingly.

"Yeah, well..." Donovan said, grinning, his eyes glittering humorously.

"Yes, well, I've yet to be shot at while making steak tartar, or baked alaska," Serena said, her tone mockingly haughty.

Donovan laughed, shaking his head. "No, I guess not. How is Paris, anyway?"

"It's wonderful, Pony, you would have loved it," she said, her eyes shining.

Before Donovan could answer, Jeanie walked out of his bathroom. She'd had the door closed so she hadn't heard Serena come in. When she saw the red-headed woman sitting next to Donovan, she stopped. She was surprised at the strength of the sudden feeling of possessiveness that came over her. She strode over to stand beside the bed, watching the other woman. Donovan's eyes went to her, then to Serena, who was watching Jeanie curiously.

"Jay," Donovan said, "this is—"

"I know who she is," Jeanie said, more sharply than she'd meant to. She smiled to try and take the bite out of her words.

"Okay…" Donovan said, not sure how to react to this side of his girlfriend, which he'd never seen. "Well, Serena, this is Jeanie…" He trailed off as Jeanie leaned past him, extending her hand perfunctorily toward Serena.

"His girlfriend," Jeanie said pointedly, as if finishing for Donovan.

Serena took Jeanie's hand almost cautiously, nodding. She did understand Jeanie's demeanor. She knew it was how she'd be acting if Donovan were still hers and another woman was hanging around him. Jeanie had something to protect. Donovan looked taken back, and Serena knew this was significant. She guessed that Jeanie knew all about her and Donovan's past and that was the reason for her strong reaction.

59

"It's nice to meet you," she said, careful to keep her tone friendly.

Jeanie simply nodded, watching her. There was an uncomfortable silence for a long few moments.

"So," Donovan said pointedly as he looked at Jeanie, his brows furrowed, then back to Serena. "You were telling me about Paris. How's the job going there?"

"It's going just fine," Serena said, relieved to be able to talk to him about something less sensitive than what was going on between his girlfriend, him, and her. "In fact I'm assistant to the head chef right now, and if my luck holds, he's considering moving on, and that would make me a shoo-in for his position."

"That's great," Donovan said, smiling broadly. "Damn, bet the Frenchies are eating their hearts out about that, huh?"

"Oh, tell me about it," Serena said, laughing. "You know, everything they told us about the French chefs is so true, Pony. They are pretentious, stuck up, and overbearing to the nth power."

"Gee, I'm really sorry I didn't get to experience that firsthand," Donovan said sarcastically, rolling his eyes and shaking his head.

"Oh, stop! By now you'd have been speaking perfect, fluent French and driving the Parisian mademoiselles crazy. I know how you are—you adapt to any environment." She looked pointedly at his shoulder then, arching an eyebrow. "Well, almost."

"Cute," Donovan countered. He could almost feel Jeanie's tension behind him. He couldn't put his arm around her, since she was on his left side and that was the shoulder that was wounded. He looked at her, lifting his left hand up from the pillow it rested on. After a long moment, Jeanie took it, sitting down next to him.

"So how is the job going? Besides this, I mean," Serena said, watching the exchange between Donovan and his girlfriend.

"Pretty good." Donovan relaxed against the pillows behind him. "I made sergeant a few months back. I'm assigned to narcotics normally, but I'm working on this special project with Midnight now."

"This house is hers, right?" Serena asked, having been told that by her brother.

"Yeah, she's letting me rent it. Kinda like family, ya know?" Donovan said, grinning.

"And the Mustang?" Serena asked. "I noted you got the plate you always wanted."

"Yeah, told you I'd have one, one day. And yeah, the plate was a plus." He realized it was probably bugging Jeanie that Serena seemed to know him so well. He and Serena had pretty much bared their souls to each other when they were together. Serena probably knew him better than Jeanie, in all actuality. It bothered him to realize that.

They talked for a while longer, but eventually it was obvious to Serena that Donovan was tired. "I better get going," she said, standing up.

"I'll walk you out," Jeanie volunteered, garnering a sharp glance from Donovan. She smiled at him, and he narrowed his eyes just slightly, pursing his lips in contemplation.

At Donovan's front door, Serena turned to look at Jeanie. "I want you to know," she said evenly, "I understand why you're so protective of Donovan."

"Good," Jeanie replied coolly.

"You should also know you have good reason to be on your

guard," Serena said simply, and with that walked out the front door. Jeanie stared after her long after the door closed behind her. She knew she'd just received a barely veiled threat, and she wasn't sure how to react. She went back to the bedroom and found that Donovan had lain down and his eyes were closed. After a moment's hesitation she climbed in beside him, sliding her hand up his stomach and chest, careful to avoid the bandages. Donovan opened his eyes, glancing down at her.

"I guess I don't need to ask how you felt about meeting Serena, huh?" he said, only half joking.

"She wants you back, Donovan," Jeanie said, looking up at him.

Donovan sighed. "Jay…"

"Don't try and tell me that she doesn't. She basically just told me she does," she said stridently.

Donovan looked surprised, but then shook his head. "Jay, her and I are over. We have been for a long time." He slid his right arm under her neck, pulling her close to him. He kissed her softly on the lips, then moved to kiss her cheek, then her ear. "Tell me how the academy went," he whispered.

Jeanie shivered at the feeling of his lips. It made her realize it had been over three weeks since they'd made love. Turning her head, she caught his lips with hers again, kissing him intensely, feeling the need to reclaim him. They kissed for a long while, both getting very warm in the process. When her hand slid too close to the bandage on his shoulder, he jumped, bringing them out of their heated embrace.

"Donovan, I'm sorry," Jeanie said, shaking her head. "We shouldn't be trying any of this, not till you're healed better. I just…" She trailed off as she shook her head again.

"I know, babe," Donovan said, looking into her eyes. "I'm in the same place, okay?"

Jeanie grinned. "What place is that?"

He grinned back. "That 'I want to do a lot more with my body right now than I'm capable of' place."

"Well, I could…" Jeanie moved her hand pointedly lower, touching the top of his sweatpants.

"You could *not*," Donovan said, his voice lowered. "I'll wait." He sounded more convincing than he felt.

Jeanie grinned. "Uh-huh."

"Come on." Donovan tried to grab her hand with his left hand and winced as he overextended his shoulder.

"Donovan, damn, I'm sorry," she said again, sounding contrite. "I'll stop now."

"Tell me about the academy," he said gently, kissing her forehead.

They spent the rest of the evening talking about the academy and what she could expect. Jeanie left his house a couple of hours later. She had to get up early for training, so she couldn't stay with him near as late anymore.

Things in Midnight's office were decidedly tense. Christian could feel her agitation and made a point of keeping quiet. He knew she wasn't happy that he knew about her condition and her subsequent battle with her husband to remain in that condition. It had been a week since she'd found out about being pregnant. Christian could tell from her demeanor that things in that arena had yet to be resolved. Matters didn't improve when Joe stormed into her office that afternoon.

Christian was sitting at Midnight's office table reading over computer printouts, and she was sitting at her desk when the door opened and Joe stepped inside.

"What the fuck are you thinking?" he asked without preamble, his light blue eyes narrowed at Midnight.

She looked up, her eyes challenging him. "I know what I'm doing," she said evenly.

"Killing yourself?"

"No, refusing to be bullied into something I don't want." Midnight's voice was irritatingly calm.

"You're not even trying to be reasonable, Night," Joe countered, moving to sit in front of her desk, glancing at Christian as he did and then to Midnight questioningly.

"Blue knows about everything," Midnight said caustically. "He was lucky enough to be in on the ground floor of all this bullshit."

"It's not bullshit, Midnight," Joe said seriously. "You need to get it done. You can't do this, and you know he's not gonna let you anyway."

"Who died and made Rick God?" Midnight asked, raising an eyebrow at her partner, then shaking her head as if not understanding him. "Rick doesn't have a choice in this matter. I'm not signing anything, and that's that."

"You're being stupid," Joe said, staring into her eyes.

Midnight shrugged. "Maybe. Guess we'll find out."

"And if you die?" Joe asked, his voice breaking on the last word.

"Then I guess you two will have been right." Midnight replied, staring back at him.

"Night…" Joe whispered, choked.

"Joe, none of us knows what would have happened last time. I know what you and Rick are thinking about, and it's not the same thing. He's thinking of the scene at the house when Keyla found me, and you're thinking about all that crap before…" She trailed off, indicating their brief affair and her subsequent near-death experience when he hadn't been there. "But it's not like that this time. It's not going to be like that," she said beseechingly, her eyes searching his.

Joe was silent for a long moment, then expelled his breath slowly, shaking his head. "We can't take that chance with you, love," he said, his voice soft but sure. "We can't lose you."

Christian watched the exchange, amazed that his cousin could feel so much for this woman and yet be married to someone else. He knew Rick was fully aware of how much Joe loved Midnight—that was what astounded him. He couldn't fathom having that kind of faith in another man, knowing that your best friend wouldn't betray your trust with what you held most sacred. Christian knew too that Midnight was what Rick held most sacred in the world. He'd gained that insight that day at the hospital, from the vehemence of Rick's concern to the look of utter terror on the man's face when his wife refused to have an abortion to save her own life. These people continued to amaze him at every turn.

That afternoon Christian picked Susan up from school. It was an odd day, since it was Friday, but she'd had a special lab. Randy had taken the day off and was home with the children. He was feeling the definite need for a drink by the time he pulled up in front of the laboratory building at the college. It had been a bad day. The conversation between Joe and Midnight notwithstanding, he was stuck on a problem with the inventory program he was developing and it was making him crazy.

Susan got into the car, glancing over at him.

"Bad day?" she asked, her tone almost friendly. They'd been on better terms since Donovan was shot, having been stuck together a lot with the children when Randy was at the hospital. Christian had also pointedly stayed close to the house since the threat to the family had come to light. They'd actually had a few civilized conversations.

"Bad enough," he said, his tone vile, as he put the car into gear and pulled away from the curb. "You got anything going on tonight?"

"No, why?"

"'Cause I need a drink," he said simply.

"And that involves me how?" she asked, raising an eyebrow at him.

He grinned. "I don't want to drink alone."

"You want me to get stuck trying to drive home if you get too drunk," she countered. He'd been trying to teach her to drive. She'd picked it up easily enough, but he was after her constantly to perfect the skill.

"Now why would I do that?" Christian replied, still grinning.

"Hmm…" Susan said, but she was interested enough in seeing him in a social situation not to argue with him.

Christian pulled up to the bar in Pacific Beach that he now frequented. Tara greeted him with a long kiss. They'd become pretty good friends by that time. Susan observed the kiss, and the way Christian and Tara talked. There were other people at the bar that night that Christian had seen a lot of times before. He talked with them, joking and laughing. Susan watched, fascinated by this side of the somber, intense man that she was used to. She had a few drinks herself at Christian's insistence. By the time they left, she was feeling a lot more drunk than he looked.

Christian had purposely bought her drinks, trying to loosen her up a little bit. He wasn't too buzzed, so he felt okay driving home. They talked about different things on the way and Christian found that she was a little drunk, and he found it amusing. She was definitely looser.

Later, Christian lay in bed, one arm cushioning his head. He was thinking about all the things that had happened since he'd arrived in America. He'd learned a lot about his cousin and the people surrounding him. It was interesting, the way the two families actually seemed to mesh into one. Midnight had been just as concerned about Donovan as Joe and Randy had. Joe was as worried about Midnight as Rick. It was certainly different for Christian; he was used to very little family and a lot of people around him he didn't trust.

As he leaned over to turn off the light, he heard a soft knock on the door.

"Come," he said, sitting back. He was wearing only black sweatpants, having been ready to go to sleep.

Susan opened the door and felt her breath catch in her throat at the sight of him. She'd been feeling very brave moments before, but even the alcohol in her system couldn't lessen the impact of seeing him bare-chested. His direct stare didn't make his incredible good looks any easier to ignore.

"What are you doing here?" he asked, his voice clear but low.

Susan hesitated, but gathering up the nerve that had brought her down to his room, she walked over to the bed. "I wanted to thank you," she said.

"For what?" he countered, his light blue eyes still staring right back into hers.

"For…" Susan began, but hesitated. Seeing the slow grin start on his face, she hurried on. "For taking me with you tonight. It was interesting to see you in a social setting. You're different there."

"Different?" Christian said, raising one jet black eyebrow at her.

"Yes," she replied, her voice softening. She sat down on the bed next to him, her eyes searching his. "You're less cool, you smile more."

"That's alcohol, love," Christian said cynically.

"No, it's not," Susan said, her voice strong. "That's what you'd like me to think. But you know what I think, Christian Collins?"

"What?" he asked, his tone indicating that he didn't care, but he was watching her eyes.

"I think you don't want anyone to see the real you. I think you have perfected that cool facade to keep people at arm's length or farther." Her eyes searched his face. "It must be difficult for you, being so handsome," she said. To Christian's surprise, he heard no jealousy or sarcasm in her tone. She sounded sincere.

"Why do you say that?" he asked, his tone still cool.

"People are always watching you, aren't they?" she asked, as if he hadn't spoken. "They're always expecting something from you. For you to act a certain way, or do a certain thing. It must be so hard to live up to standards that you had nothing to do with setting. It's like trying to play a game without knowing the rules, or even understanding the game itself." She sounded so sincere that Christian felt himself involuntarily responding, softening his own tone.

"It's always the golden rules, love," he said, sounding cynical and wise, as he shook his head. "Their gold, their rules." His eyes reflected a look of such calm acceptance that it made Susan want to touch him, to change things for him. She'd never seen him actually look vulnerable, not even for a moment. It affected her more than she wanted to admit.

"And they always wanted something from you, didn't they?" she asked, her eyes reflecting remorse at the thought.

"They wanted what they saw," Christian replied, his tone indicating his distaste for what he was saying.

"And that's what you gave them?" she asked, surprised.

Christian nodded, his eyes taking on a knowing look. "People get what they pay for," he said coldly.

"And that's okay with you?" Susan was sure she knew the answer, even when he shrugged nonchalantly, looking back at her coolly. "I think you're lying," she said, her voice a whisper as if to take the sting out of her words. "I think that trading on your looks is something you've done, but I don't think you like it, not for one minute."

"What makes you think that?" Christian said softly, his eyes still holding hers intently.

"Because I think there's so much more to you than a gorgeous face. I think you hate having to use the one thing that was God-given, because it makes you less significant that way. But you can't turn it off, can you?"

"Turn what off?" he asked, his expression changing slightly.

"People's attraction to you, it's magnetic. I saw it tonight—people want to be around you even when you're cold as ice. I'll bet your anger draws people in even closer, doesn't it?"

Christian stared back at her, his light blue eyes reflecting surprise. He was remembering his last confrontation with Geneva, and Susan was right—his anger had only served to excite her more.

"So," he said, sitting up and resting his elbow on the pillows next to him. He propped his head up on his fist, staring into her eyes. "What else do you *think* about me?" They were on an even level now; he was closer than before, and Susan felt affected by that.

She swallowed, trying to find her voice. "I think you've never been in a situation like this, where people expect to know more about you, and I think it scares the hell out of you." A grin tugged at his lips, but he said nothing, forcing her to continue. "I also think you're in for a shock when you realize that we *don't* expect anything from you."

"But what do you *want*?" Christian asked, emphasizing the difference between expectation and desire.

"I want…" Susan began, her voice almost breathless because the look in his eyes had changed and she knew they were talking on two different levels now. "I want for you to let someone in, to trust someone enough to be yourself, your real self."

70

"And you don't think this is me?"

"No," she answered simply.

"So how would you know the real me?" he asked, a grin playing at his lips.

"Show me," she replied, knowing she was talking about more than his true self.

Without a word he leaned in, closing the distance between them, his lips taking possession of hers almost hungrily. He pulled her close to him. Susan responded to his kiss, clutching at his arms as if to keep from falling. Her body melted against his as a low moan escaped her lips. He pulled away from her just enough to look down at her.

"What do you want me to show you?" he asked, his voice a husky whisper.

"What are you good at?" she countered, surprising herself with her bravado.

"Everythin'," he replied, his voice strong and confident.

"Then show me everything," she whispered.

His lips came down on hers again, his arms pulling her body flush with his. He slid his hands up her back, his fingers clutching at the material of her blouse and pulling it free of her skirt and over her head a moment later. He removed the rest of her clothing with equal swiftness. Sitting back, he looked down at her, a wry grin on his face as he shook his head.

"I knew it," he said huskily. "I knew you were hiding a body under all that crap." He gestured to her clothes lying on the floor. "And now…" He reached up and behind her, tugging at the pins that held her hair up. Pulling the last one free, Christian watched, fascinated, as her honey-blond hair tumbled more than halfway to her waist. He drew in his breath, his eyes reflecting his appreciation of her appearance.

"You have all this," he said, taking a handful of her hair and rubbing it gently between his fingers. "And you tie it up like that all the time?" His voice reflected his lack of understanding.

"Long hair is not conducive to children," Susan said, her voice indicating her desire.

"There are no children here," Christian said, taking on a possessive tone. His lips covered hers again, making her burn.

Before moving to lie back on the bed, Christian slid off his jeans and then pulled her down with him and onto her side, so that they faced each other. He moved his hands smoothly over her skin, tugging at her hips to draw her closer to him still. He moved his legs possessively over hers as he looked down at her.

When he spoke his voice was a caressing whisper, the voice of a lover. It made Susan shiver, but his words made her body tingle with anticipation.

"Making love is all about communication," he said, sliding his hand from her waist, up her body, to touch her face gently. "It's all about action and reaction. If I do something you like, you have to show me you like it."

"How?" Susan whispered.

"With your hands," he said, moving his hand to her shoulder and grasping it gently, as if to demonstrate. "With your voice," he said, his voice lowering an octave. "Or with your body," he said, moving impossibly closer to her. Susan could feel the heat between them, and could only imagine things to come. She nodded, showing him that she understood.

"Now," he said, pinning her with a look as his voice became firmer with admonition, "this is about touch, taste, and feel. I want you to *feel* this, Susan. Don't try to think. Forget about everything. Nothing else matters but here and now, this room, this bed, our bodies, no one else, nothing else. Okay?" His expression told her he was serious, and again she nodded, understanding what he meant.

"Just be here with *me*, now," Christian said.

He lowered his head then, his lips grazing her shoulder, making her shudder. He kissed her, moving his lips down her collarbone to the base of her throat, caressing her skin with his hand all the while.

She slid her hands up his back, clutching at his shoulder, unconsciously digging her nails into the muscle. Christian gasped at the sensation.

"What?" Susan asked, not sure what she'd done.

"Your nails," Christian said huskily.

"I don't have any," Susan said, considering her short nails insignificant.

"No, you have them, just enough. I can still feel your fingertips," he said, his voice decidedly excited. "I like it." His lips were against her neck as he spoke, and then he began to kiss her again.

He pushed her down so she lay on her back, sliding his hands from her thigh, up over her stomach and just to the side of her breasts. Susan could feel them leaving a warm trail of tingling nerves in their wake.

"You have the most incredible skin," he said, his lips next to her ear. He began kissing her neck, and as he moved lower, he literally

73

moved her up, his strong hands holding her by the waist.

When his lips touched her breasts, Susan cried out, her hands burying themselves in his hair. She shuddered when she felt his tongue touch her skin, the sensations he was causing making her writhe with desire.

"Christian…" she said, her voice leaden with wanting.

Christian felt himself respond intensely. He increased his fervor, which caused Susan to clutch blindly at his shoulder as she felt her body spinning out of control.

"Christian, Christian," she said over and over, her voice still holding its passionate timbre. It made him have to fight for control of his own body.

"That's it," he said, his voice almost harsh with barely controlled passion.

"What?" she asked, trying to grasp at anything to keep from exploding at that moment.

"The way you say my name when you want me, it drives me crazy," he said, his voice indicating he very much meant it.

"I do want you, Christian, now… right now… please…" she said, her desire making her more brazen as she slid down his body so she could kiss his lips.

Christian rolled to his back, pulling her over him, and in one fluid movement slid her body down on his, his body entering hers easily. Susan gasped at the new sensation. She had never been as ready for a man as she was at that moment, her body screaming for the pressure of his body inside hers. Her lovemaking with Warren didn't even come within miles of what she was feeling now. The sensation was so different, so much more intense and stronger, like a driving need.

He grasped her waist, urging her body ever closer and harder down on his. Within minutes they were both exclaiming in their release, their hands clutching at each other.

Afterward, they lay trying to catch their breath. Susan lay over him, her head resting on his chest, her breath coming in ragged gasps. He stroked her hair and back as he lay with his eyes closed. After a few long minutes, Susan started to move to disengage herself. Christian's hands held her fast.

"Don't," he said, his voice still reflecting the effects of their lovemaking. Susan didn't argue with him—she didn't want to, she enjoyed the closeness to him, and the idea that he wanted her where she was.

They stayed that way for a long time, but eventually he shifted her so she lay next to him. He held her close. He turned to face her after a while, watching her. She looked up at him, the look in her eyes cautious, not sure how he would be now. He surprised her by bending his head to kiss her softly on the lips again. When they parted, she laid her head in the hollow of his shoulder, reveling in the warmth of his embrace. This was not what she had expected. When he had taunted her about his earlier excitation of her senses being the beginning, she had assumed he'd been exaggerating. He hadn't.

Christian lay with his eyes closed, from all outward appearances calm. Inside he was reeling. It had been years since his body had responded so fiercely to a woman. It had also been years since he had felt the need to stay close to a woman afterward. But with Susan he found that both were the case. He had taken a totally different approach to making love to her as well, something he was not given to doing. He didn't know if it was her words or her unabashed response to him that had spurred him to greater heights.

He slept for a while, feeling sated and comfortable. When he woke a couple of hours later, he felt her hand on his cheek. He opened his eyes and looked down at her. She didn't take her hand away, though she did move it to stroke his hair, her nails grazing his scalp. Christian watched her, but was surprised at his reaction to an action that he normally abhorred as too affectionate, too close. Instead of being irritated by it, he felt a desire to have her touch him more. It bothered him remotely that this was yet another difference with her. But even as the thought needled at him, his body responded to its own desire. He moved onto his back, his arm under her neck pulling her close again, his hand caressing her back. When she hesitated he took her hand in his, guiding it to his chest, pressing it flat against the muscles there. She looked at him for a long moment, her eyes widening slightly.

"What do you want to do, Zan?" he asked softly, shortening her name, an endearment not lost on her even as his words sent a thrill through her.

"I want…" she said quietly, her eyes dropping from his in her hesitation.

"What?" he asked gently.

"To touch you," she said, sounding as if she was afraid he'd be angry.

"Zan," he said, more strongly now. "That's what I want too. Do it." His voice was a husky whisper on the last.

76

Gathering her nerve, Susan slid her hand over his chest, flexing her fingers so her nails grazed his skin. She shivered when he drew a sharp breath, his hand at her back gripping her tighter. His reaction to her touch spurred her to more seductive measures, wanting to elicit his response. She slid her hand downward and heard his low groan. She was above him on the pillows, so when he turned his head his lips pressed into the hollow between her breasts. Pulling her closer to him, he buried his face against her, inhaling deeply.

"You smell so goddamned good," he whispered against her skin. She smelled like jasmine, and the scent was intoxicating. His lips trailed down her torso as his hands caressed her. She clutched at his back, her nails digging into his skin, spurring him on. When he could stand it no longer he moved over her, making love to her, taking them both to all new heights.

They ended up staying together the entire night. Susan woke lying in his arms the following morning. She watched him sleep, feeling like her whole world had been turned upside down. He was such an incredible-looking man. She couldn't even begin to understand what had happened between them. She did know that she had felt more with him in one night than she'd felt with Warren all along.

When he woke, he looked down at her, watching her eyes carefully.

"Good morning," she whispered, not sure what to say. "I didn't know if I should—" she began, but his lips on hers stopped her. He kissed her until she was breathless, and then pulled back to look down at her, his light blue eyes searching hers, as if trying to see if she understood him.

"You don't want to talk," Susan said softly.

Christian grinned, his eyes half closing as he looked down at her. "Very good," he said lightly. He moved to kiss her again, and within minutes they were tightly entwined as their bodies responded to each other. "Jesus…" Christian whispered against her lips.

"What?" Susan asked, incited by his tone.

"I can't believe how much I want you again. With most women, I'm done wanting them before I've even finished having them… but you… God…" His voice was strained as he fought to control his body, and Susan couldn't help but be excited by it. He kissed her again, and after a long few minutes brought his hand up to her face. He pulled back, looking down at her, caressing her cheek. He brought his lips back down to hers, and then whispered against them, "Give me your tongue."

"What?" Susan whispered, not sure what he meant.

"Bring your tongue out to touch mine. I'll show you…" he said softly, but his voice held an instructional tone.

She did as he said, and felt his tongue touch hers as he kissed her again. After a few moments he closed his mouth over her tongue, sucking on it gently, making her groan at the sensation it caused. Then he slid his tongue seductively over her lips, slipping past them to touch her tongue again. He pulled back again, looking down at her. This time Susan moved to kiss him, using her tongue as he had, making him groan this time.

"You learn damn quick," Christian said, shaking his head.

"Tell me how to excite you, Christian," Susan said, her voice an urgent whisper.

"You do."

"But I want to really excite you, like you do me," Susan countered, surprising herself with her boldness.

"Then you have to figure out what excites me," Christian said, using the distraction of their conversation to bring his body under control.

He moved onto his back, pulling her over him. Susan looked down at him, her face serious, but her eyes sparkling.

"How do I do that?" she asked cautiously. She didn't want to make him angry, but she really wanted to know how to get to him. She was guessing that he didn't want her to know.

"That, love, is the trick," he said, his voice still holding an instructional tone. "You have to try things, test things. Not everything works the same on everyone."

"But what works on you?"

"Find out," he said, his tone challenging now.

Susan looked at him for a long moment, then lowered her head to his chest and kissed it. She moved to his neck. His hands on her back clutched at her, his fingertips digging into her skin as he moaned softly. Susan pulled back and looked down at him. His light blue eyes burned with desire.

"I guess that was one thing," she said, grinning.

"I guess…" Christian echoed.

"Am I going to have to track down the other women you've been with to uncover all the mysteries to you?" Susan asked, narrowing her eyes.

He shrugged. "Wouldn't help."

"Why not?" She was surprised that he was even talking to her about all this.

"Because I'm different with different women."

"Why?"

"Because the women are different. Like you," he said, kissing her softly on the lips. "Some of the women I've been with have lots of experience at this, so a lot of things they do don't excite me. But you... you're pretty new at this, so when you do something different, it excites me. 'Cause I know that I've brought that out of you. You're different with me, and I like that."

"But you're different too, aren't you?" Susan asked, her voice a whisper. She knew she was asking too many questions and that any minute now he'd shut down and stop talking to her.

Christian was silent for a long moment, then a slow grin started on his face.

"You don't want me to know that, do you?" she asked, pinpointing exactly what he was thinking. "You want me to think that I'm like every other woman you've been with... but I'm not, am I?"

"No," Christian said finally, shaking his head.

"How am I different? Why?" Susan wasn't sure if it was a bad thing or not.

"This," he said, gesturing to her body over his. "I never want to feel a woman against me, like I want you against me. Your skin is like silk and I just want it close to me. And... I've never wanted a woman as often as I've wanted you in the last so many hours." He slid his hand up her back, pulling her head down to kiss her deeply, feeling her hands flex against his chest. "You react to me like no one I've ever been with," he said, pulling back to look at her. "And believe me, they

80

react to me all the time. But you don't hold back, you don't try to pretend like I don't get to you."

"You do get to me. But I want to excite you," Susan said, coming back to her original desire. "What do you like?"

"I like your hands on my skin. I like your lips on my neck, I like the feel of your hair on…" He trailed off as she pulled back just enough that her hair fell over his chest, as if she knew what he had been about to say. He closed his eyes, caressing her back. "You affect me much more than I want you to, Zan," he said, thinking he was stupid for telling her all of this.

Susan looked at him, surprised; she thought it was just the opposite. But then she decided to test out this new power. She lowered her head to his chest again and kissed him, moving her lips up to his neck, taking her time. She could feel him responding, his breathing becoming heavier, his hands grasping at her back. It excited her no end. She lay half over him, her hair falling to brush his chest, torso, and stomach. She slid her body upward and began kissing his lips hungrily, her own need starting to burn in her. Christian surprised her by putting his hands on her waist and lifting her away from him then sliding her body further upward so that his lips grazed her breasts. Susan gasped at the feeling, bending her head to his, her lips against his hair.

"God, Christian," she gasped, holding his head against her, writhing with desire for him. After a few minutes he lowered her back down his body, but not entering her as she'd expected him to. "Christian, please…" she whispered against his neck, clutching at his shoulders.

"I can feel your heat against me, Zan. Let it go," he said, moving to kiss her neck, actually nipping lightly at her skin with his teeth, which set her on fire again instantly. His arm wrapped around her waist began moving her rhythmically against his leg, making her moan. She slid her hands from his shoulder, allowing her nails to trail across his skin, making him shudder. He slid his tongue up her neck to just behind her ear. "Let it go, Zan," he whispered against her ear. Susan shook her head, just slightly, not wanting to orgasm without him.

It became a battle then, each of them trying to make the other lose control. Before long neither of them was thinking clearly. "Zan, Zan…" Christian was chanting, holding her tightly against him with one arm, his other hand buried in her hair, caressing her neck, and every so often using a handful of her hair to guide her lips back to his. "Damn it, damn it…" he said, feeling himself losing the battle, and she hadn't even allowed her hand to travel down to the danger zone yet. He knew if she did, he was gone…

Susan couldn't think of anything but Christian, the feeling of his hands on her, the taste of his lips, the scent of Havana cologne still on his skin, and the heat between them. She knew that she could easily give in and let herself orgasm, but she wanted him to have one as well, feeling like she needed some power over him. She was determined not to lose this mindless battle.

"God, Zan… God…" Christian said, his body tensing against hers.

"I want you to let go, Christian," Susan said, her lips at his ear, feeling his breath against the side of her face.

"Then touch me," he said, finally giving her the key to getting to him as he guided her hand downward. As her hand closed over him, he bit down on the sensitive part of her neck, sucking at her skin, making her groan and cry out at the sudden pressure and the excitement of what they were doing. They reached their climax together, and lay a few minutes later gasping for breath.

Susan rested her head in the hollow between his neck and shoulder. She felt him shaking his head. "What?" she asked, without raising her head.

"You're the first woman to ever manage that with me," he said huskily.

Now Susan did lift her head, staring at him in amazement. "Really?" she asked, surprised by his admission.

"Yeah… I never let anyone else get that close for that long," he said, again thinking he was being foolish this particular day.

Susan didn't reply. She lay back down against him and stroked his chest.

After a long few minutes he asked, "What do you have going on today?"

"It's my day off."

"Then stay here with me, in bed, all day," he said, emphasizing where they'd be to indicate what he intended to be doing. Susan nodded against his chest, kissing his neck.

Things between Rick and Midnight erupted that weekend. Midnight slept most of the day on Saturday, waking to find Rick in the chair next to their bed. He had one jean-clad knee up to his chest, his arms hugging that leg as his chin rested on his knee, watching her with his deep blue eyes. Midnight found herself thinking how incredible-looking he still was. Even at thirty-four Rick still looked like he had when they met. His lean, finely boned face was still as smooth as ever, his lean swimmer's body was still strong without an ounce of fat on it. His light brown hair was still long and curly, reaching a good three inches past his shoulders. He could still turn her on with a look, and drive her absolutely mad with his lips, hands, and body. Unfortunately, he could also still make her mad enough to chew nails, and want to scream and hit something, him most of the time.

She'd only made that mistake once, however. They'd been fighting about her ability to protect herself on a raid. He'd taunted her over and over that she couldn't hack it anymore, but he'd pushed the wrong button and it had culminated in her launching herself at him, punching him in the face. He had staggered back, narrowing his eyes at her dangerously. Midnight had stepped back, immediately looking stricken. He'd terrified her by actually taking a step toward her, his arm tensing. Midnight had stood her ground, fully expecting him to hit her back. Rick had stopped, closing his eyes and swallowing against the anger that had flooded his veins.

He'd left the room then, and she'd found him out on their deck an hour later getting drunk. She'd taken the bottle from his hand and reached up to touch the bruise on his cheek. He had stared back at her with no emotion in his deep blue eyes, but Midnight had gone on undaunted, willing to do anything to make it up to him.

She'd kissed his cheek, moving back to his ear, and whispered, "I'm sorry, babe. I love you."

Then she'd proceeded to show him just how much. Eventually he'd relaxed in her embrace and begun to kiss her back. Later they'd lain together in bed and talked about the incident. He'd made her fully aware of the fact that she'd gone over the line, and she had assured him that she knew that. He'd also told her that he'd always known she could hit, but now he guessed he really knew. She'd never made the mistake of hitting him again, fearful that the next time he would hit her back—and she'd seen him knock Joe down. She didn't relish the idea of ever being on the receiving end of one of his punches.

Now, as she looked at him, she knew they were about to fight. It made her stomach tighten, which subsequently made her feel like throwing up. Which she promptly went into their bathroom and did. As she came back into the room, Rick watched her. Midnight lay back down on the bed, ignoring his brooding stare.

"When are you going to give up this stupid idea?" Rick asked, sighing.

Midnight narrowed her eyes at him. "In about five and half months," she said simply, making him draw in a sharp breath. She'd graphically reminded him that she had only a two-week window until having an abortion would be dangerous for her as well.

"Damn it, Night!" he said, his anger driving him to his feet.

"Rick," Midnight sighed, "we've been through this."

"Yes, and we're still not where I want to be," Rick said stridently. "So we're going through it again."

"No, I'm not." Midnight sat up, looking extremely tired. "You can talk all you want, but I'm not having an abortion, and that's it."

"And if it kills you?" Rick asked, looking stricken.

Midnight looked back at him for a long moment, then shrugged. "It's a chance I'm willing to take."

Rick stood staring at her for a long moment, feeling anger flood his veins. "When did you get so fucking selfish?" he raged, his accent thicker with his angst.

Midnight didn't answer him. She simply looked back at him, her face a calm mask. Inside she was having to fight the wave of nausea that was welling in her again. She knew it was because she was tense. She hated fighting with him, but she knew that what she was fighting for was worth it.

"Midnight," Rick said, moving to the bed and sitting down in front of her, taking her hands in his as he looked down into her eyes. "Don't do this to yourself, to us... to me." His voice was quiet and strained.

"I'm doing this for us, for you," Midnight said quietly. "I want this baby—your baby."

"Damn it!" Rick yelled, sitting back. "Don't do that. Don't make me the reason you're killing yourself. 'Cause I don't want this baby, not if it means losing you."

"It's not your decision to make," Midnight said, closing down again. Rick could almost see the wall drop between them.

Without stopping to think, he grabbed her by the shoulder and dragged her over to him. He kissed her, trying to keep her from shutting off. He felt her resist instantly; she knew him well enough to know his tactics.

"Damn it, Midnight," he grated against her lips. "If you love me you won't do this."

He'd pulled his trump card, and he knew he was walking a dangerous line. He felt her hands on his chest, and was surprised when she shoved him away with more force than he would have believed her capable of. He fell back, hitting his head against the dresser behind him, and then dropped to the floor. He stared up at her, seeing the anger on her face, and knew he'd pushed her too far this time.

He reached up, touching the back of his head gingerly. Pulling his hand away, he saw blood. Again he looked up at her, and saw that she was staring at his hand. Then her eyes trailed up to his. The look on her face told him she didn't plan to discuss this with him any longer. Rick expelled his breath, closing his eyes and leaning back against the dresser. He sat with his knees up to his chest, feeling his stomach churning. He knew there was nothing he could say to make her change her mind; he knew she was as stubborn as he'd be if it was something he believed in.

There had been many times in their nine-year marriage that Rick had railed at the fates for making him fall in love with a woman that could be as impossible as she was incredible. They had spent those nine years constantly butting heads over any number of issues, but never one that left him feeling like he had to change her mind, no matter what it cost him. This was that exception, and Rick wasn't sure what he was going to do to achieve that.

"Dad," said a small voice. Rick turned his head and saw Mikeyla standing in the doorway, looking very worried.

"Keyl," he said, knowing she had heard them arguing. Mikeyla walked into the room, moving to kneel beside him.

"Daddy, you're bleeding," she said, her voice shrill with worry.

"I know, baby. It's okay, I just hit my head. I'm alright," Rick said, not wanting his daughter upset now too. He stood up to show her how "okay" he was and found that his head was pounding mightily. He sat down on the bed with his back to Midnight.

Mikeyla noted the tension between her parents and looked at her mother. Midnight had moved to sit against the headboard, her head back against the pillows.

"What's going on?" Mikeyla asked, sounding suspicious. "Why are you fighting?" It always worried her when her parents fought. No matter how often they assured her they would never break up again, she was always concerned that that was exactly what they'd do.

Neither Midnight nor Rick answered her. Mikeyla looked at each of them, her eyes wide with worry. Finally, Rick couldn't stand it anymore. "It's okay, Keyl," he said calmly.

"What are you fighting about?" Mikeyla repeated, not willing to be put off.

This time she looked at her mother, her eyes narrowed. Mikeyla had turned into the epitome of a daddy's girl; she always favored Rick, and when it came to arguments she usually assumed her mother was just being difficult. She had no idea how right she was this time.

Rick said nothing for a long moment, then turned to Midnight, pinning her with a look. "Tell her," he said seriously.

Midnight narrowed her eyes at him, then looked at her daughter. She took a deep breath and gestured for her to sit down. Mikeyla did, sitting between her parents on the bed.

"Well," Midnight began, feeling her irritation rise as she noted that Rick was watching her, his handsome face set in an arrogant mask. "You know I've been a little sick lately, right?" Mikeyla nodded, glancing at her father as if looking for clues to what her mother was about to tell her. "Well, the thing is, I'm not sick... I'm pregnant." Midnight said the last in almost a whisper.

Mikeyla looked back at her mother, stunned. "You're..." she

said, her voice trailing off. She suddenly looked as stricken as her father had minutes before.

"Keyl," Midnight said, reaching out to touch her daughter's hand. "Look, it's okay."

"No, Midnight," Rick said, his voice strong. "Don't do that to her. Tell her all of it."

Midnight looked at Rick, her eyes blazing at him, but she didn't say anything more.

"Do it," Rick warned. "Or I will."

Mikeyla glanced at her father, and when she saw the look on his face, tears started in her eyes immediately.

"Okay, look," Midnight said, her tone softening. "The doctors don't think I can have this baby, but they also didn't think I could get pregnant again."

"Don't lie to her," Rick said, his voice deepening.

"I'm not lying to her, Richard. I'm telling her the whole thing, not just the dire stuff you and Joe keep chanting over me," Midnight countered, using his full name in her anger. She looked at her daughter again. "No, Keyl, I know that you're thinking about last time, and I know that scares you, but last time was very different. Last time I was hurt, and it had nothing to do with the miscarriage. That doesn't mean that will happen again—"

"Goddamn it, Midnight!" Rick raged, unable to listen anymore. "Keyl, what she's not saying is that the doctors have told her that she shouldn't even try to have this baby. In fact, the doctor wanted her to terminate the pregnancy that day." He looked at Midnight, his eyes speaking volumes about the torment he'd been going through in the last weeks. "Having this baby could very well kill her."

Mikeyla looked from her father to her mother, the tears in her eyes spilling over at his words.

"Keyl," Midnight said, throwing Rick a vile look. "They don't know anything for sure."

"But they could be right?" Mikeyla asked, concerned.

Midnight hesitated for a long moment, but nodded, not able to lie to her daughter. Mikeyla started shaking her head, her tears coming unbidden now. "No, Mom, no…" she whispered.

"Keyl—" Midnight began.

Mikeyla cut her off, screaming, "No!"

Rick put his arms around her, pulling her close and looking at Midnight over her head. Midnight looked back at him, the beginnings of tears in her own eyes. Mikeyla turned in the circle of her father's arms, looking at her mother. "Mom, please don't do this. Please…"

Midnight felt like she'd just been hit by a bulldozer. "Don't you want a baby brother or sister?" she asked, hoping to appeal to her daughter's mothering side.

"Not if it means losing you," Mikeyla said, shaking her head. "I need you, Mom, not a baby brother. Please don't do this." With that Mikeyla moved to hug her mother, and this time Midnight couldn't stop the tears that started to flow.

"Okay, baby, okay…" she crooned, stroking her daughter's hair and rocking back and forth.

"Promise me, Mom. Promise me that you won't do this," Mikeyla said, her voice muffled because her face was buried in her mother's hair. Midnight closed her eyes, feeling the impact of her daughter's fear. She opened her eyes, looking at Rick, and saw the look of self-righteousness in his expression. She narrowed her eyes, but said nothing to him.

"Okay, Keyl, okay," she said, sighing, knowing she couldn't fight both of them and not willing to let her daughter suffer for five and half months to see if she'd live through the pregnancy.

After a few minutes, Midnight told Mikeyla to leave her and Daddy alone for a bit, that they needed to talk. Rick could sense Midnight's anger even before Mikeyla closed the door. When he turned to look at her, he saw the fire burning in her eyes. He said nothing, knowing she would go through with the abortion now and feeling relieved for it.

"I will never forgive you for putting me through that," Midnight said, her voice cold even as her green eyes burned. "And I hate you for making me do this." With that said, she stood up, went into the bathroom, and closed the door.

Rick heard the shower start and the radio blast. What he didn't hear was his wife throwing up over and over, and the tears that she cried for what she was going to have to do now. Instead he sat on their bed, feeling very cold. The tone of her voice and the look in her eyes had scared him. He sat staring at the spot where she'd sat minutes before, feeling the impact of what had just happened.

He was relieved that she was going to terminate the pregnancy now, but her tangible anger had shaken his confidence in their marriage. He didn't like the thought one bit. Eventually he lay down on the bed, feeling his head throbbing from the collision with the dresser. He closed his eyes, trying to push aside memories of his and

Midnight's near divorce five years before. The memory of receiving her wedding ring in the mail at his parents' home in England still seemed so fresh in his mind. The palm of his hand still bore the scars from when he had closed it over the emerald ring, so tightly the stone had cut into his hand. The memories of Midnight's attack, miscarriage, and near death were so tightly bound to that time in his life, it made him physically sick to think about it again. He turned over on the bed, pressing his face into the pillows. Ironically, he was on her side of the bed and could smell the scent of her perfume, her hair, and just her in general. He stayed that way even when he heard Midnight come out of the bathroom. He heard her moving about the room, and heard her keys as she picked them up. Rick sat up then, looking over to where she stood, fully clothed and wearing her FORS jacket.

"What're you doing?" he asked, his voice coming out in a hoarse whisper.

"I'm doing what you want so badly," she said coldly.

"What?" he said, moving to get off the bed.

Midnight put her hand up in a halting gesture. "I don't want you there," she said sternly.

"I don't fucking care. I'm gonna be there." He stood and reached for his shoes.

"Then drive yourself," Midnight said, and walked out of the room. Rick stared after her for a long moment, not believing her intention. He heard her Corvette start up a minute later.

"Shit," he said to himself, knowing this was just the beginning of the hell she was going to put him through for this. *As long as she's alive to hate me*, he thought.

Later, when Rick arrived home he was irritated to see Midnight's Corvette in the garage. He'd spent the last five hours trying to find her. He'd gone to Mercy Hospital but was told that she'd never come there. He'd feared the worst then, that in her furious state she'd gotten into an accident. After contacting the department and Highway Patrol he found that no car matching his wife's had been involved in an accident. Rick had proceeded to check other hospitals in hopes he would catch up to her. Arriving home to find her car in the garage made him angry. He knew she liked to have him at a disadvantage, and now she did. He had no idea where she'd gone or if she'd done what she'd said she was going to do.

Feeling tense, Rick walked into the house and proceeded to their bedroom. He found Midnight lying on the bed. She wore the same shirt she'd had on when she left, and she was curled into a ball.

"Where the hell have you been?" he asked.

Midnight opened her eyes and looked up at him, her face a cool mask. "Doing what I said I'd do," she said calmly.

"Then what are you doing home so soon?" he asked, not believing her.

Midnight sat up, looking disturbingly good with her copper-blond hair flowing loose around her. Her catlike green eyes were narrowed at him, and he knew he was about to get cut to the core.

"Teenagers do these kinds of things and go back to school an hour later, Richard," she said icily. "What'd you expect? An extended stay?"

"Where did you go?" he asked, his own eyes narrowed now. He didn't like the way she was acting. He knew she hadn't seen her own doctor.

93

Midnight shrugged. "What does it matter? It's been taken care of—that's all you care about, isn't it?" Her tone was cutting, and without waiting for him to answer she lay back down, turning her back on him.

"No, that's not all I care about, Midnight," Rick said sharply, moving to sit on the bed behind her. "You matter to me, and I want to fucking know where you had it done."

Midnight didn't answer, which made him angrier.

"Tell me where you had it done," Rick said, his voice low and threatening now.

"Go piss up a rope," Midnight shot back, not one to be intimidated by Rick.

"I want to know, and you're going to tell me." Rick took her arm and forcibly turned her to face him.

"If you're so concerned," Midnight said coolly, "the paperwork is in my jacket pocket." She gestured at her FORS jacket hanging over the back of the wingback chair next to the bed. With that said, she turned back on her side, ignoring him again.

Rick reached into her jacket and pulled out the hastily folded papers.

"You went to a fucking clinic?" he asked when he'd finished checking out the documents. "How could you be so goddamned dumb?"

"My choice," Midnight replied, her tone still icy.

"Your stupid choice, Midnight. Are you trying to get yourself killed? You know as much as I do about those places—they're never sterile and half the time the doctor isn't even a real MD."

94

"Yeah, well, it's done now, so deal with it," Midnight said inscrutably.

Rick stared at her back for a long time, trying to think of something to say to make her understand how crazy what she had done was. Finally, he got up and left the room. He spent the next few hours getting quietly drunk. He couldn't believe he and Midnight were in this place again. He wondered if he'd managed to destroy his marriage, regardless of his intentions. He sincerely hoped not.

CHAPTER 3

Donovan was tired of waiting around for Jeanie. After being in bed so long, laid up with his gunshot wound, he just couldn't take it anymore. He'd seen less and less of her. She always told him that the academy was requiring more of her time than she'd expected. He'd seen her twice since the night he came home from the hospital. Both times she'd stayed an hour and then left. He knew things were all but over with her at that point, but he really didn't want to face it.

A month after being shot, Donovan drove into the department parking lot and went to see Midnight. He was told by Cassandra that the chief was out of the office that day, "sick." Donovan was surprised—Midnight never got sick. He stuck his head in her office and noted that Christian was there working on her computer. Not sure why, he walked in and sat down. Christian glanced up; he looked surprised.

"Back a little soon, aren't you?" Christian asked, his tone cool.

"Yeah, maybe, but I can't stay at home forever. Gotta get back," Donovan said, looking anything but enthusiastic.

"I guess. How's Jeanie doin' in the academy?"

"Why do you ask?" Donovan said, too defensively.

"Uh-oh, trouble in paradise?" Christian asked, a knowing grin on his face.

"Nothing I'm gonna talk to you about," Donovan shot back.

Christian nodded. "So it is a problem with our fair maiden then."

"Fuck you, Blue," Donovan said, his eyes narrowing.

"Touchy, touchy," Christian said, almost gleefully. "So what's goin' on?"

Donovan looked back at Joe's cousin for a long moment, knowing he shouldn't tell the guy anything. Finally, he shrugged. "I don't know, she's been weird ever since I was shot."

"Give 'er time, she'll get back round to you," Christian said, his tone sincere for once.

"Yeah, well she hasn't officially left either."

Christian nodded, not sure what he could say. He hadn't talked to Jeanie in a number of days either. They'd actually become pretty good friends. Jeanie knew about his favorite habit of baiting people and had made a point of avoiding falling for it. It had become a good joke between them. He always made passes, and she always dodged them.

Donovan left Midnight's office and headed to his desk in narcotics. He worked the entire morning trying to clear up his incoming mail and other minor issues. He needed to talk to Midnight about how she wanted to proceed on the case he was working for her, and with her out he couldn't do that. Donovan was surprised when someone walked up behind him and tapped him on the shoulder. He jumped a little because it was the shoulder that had been wounded. Turning around, he was very surprised to see Serena standing there. He hadn't seen or heard from her since the night she'd shown up at his house. He figured she'd gone back to Paris by that time.

"Hi," he said, smiling. "What are you doing here?"

97

"I was in the neighborhood, and I thought you might like to have lunch or something."

Donovan glanced at his watch. "Wow, I didn't realize it was that late already." He stood up. "Let's go."

It was strange for him to be walking out to his car with Serena. It was like an old scene playing in his head, but with newer objects in it.

"So," Serena said, eyeing the Mustang appreciatively, "is this car everything you ever dreamed it would be?"

Donovan grinned—she remembered well. "Yeah, it is," he said as he opened the door for her.

As they drove off, Serena laughed. "You still drive like a bat out of hell," she said, grinning all the while.

"Yeah, but now I don't get as many tickets," Donovan replied, grinning back.

"So it's true that police officers don't give other police officers tickets?"

"Most of the time. But sometimes you get the occasional asshole Highway Patrol guy who hates the PD, or some sheriff with a beef, and then you do get a ticket. I've been lucky so far."

"So how do they know you're a police officer?" Serena asked, curious about his new career.

"My plates come back cold."

"Huh?" Serena looked blank.

"Oops," Donovan said, his expression apologetic. "Sorry, forgot I was talking to a civilian. Cold plates are plates where the registration comes back to the department, not my private address."

"Oh…" Serena said, nodding as if trying to understand. "Are all police officers' registrations cold?" she asked, stammering on the lingo a bit.

"No, I've got a special status because one, I'm narcotics, and two, I'm working for the chief right now on a special project."

"And Midnight Chevalier is the chief now, right?" Serena asked, remembering what one of her brothers had told her.

"Yeah."

At a red light, Donovan reached back and under his jacket with his right arm to scratch the still-healing scar on his back. The bullet that had almost hit him in the heart had thankfully gone all the way through, leaving a nasty hole but no bullet to remove. Serena glanced over.

"Do that again," she said, looking at him strangely.

Donovan glanced over at her, not sure what she was talking about. "What?"

Serena reached over and pulled the side of the garment open, revealing what she thought she'd seen before. She was looking at his holstered gun.

"Wow," she said, shaking her head.

Donovan caught her drift and laughed. "Cops carry guns, Rena," he said, automatically using his old nickname for her.

"Yes, but… I never pictured you with a gun." Serena surprised him by reaching over and lifting the jacket away again, inspecting the holstered weapon closer. Then she noticed the gold shield clipped next to the gun. "Nice badge," she said cryptically.

Donovan reached down and unclipped it, then handed it to her.

She studied it intently.

"Sergeant," she said, reading the emblazoned title.

Donovan grinned. "Yep."

Serena handed back the badge and he slid it back onto his belt.

"I can't say I really like your new career, Pony," she said, shaking her head.

"Sorry," he replied. "I like it—it's interesting."

"Getting shot is interesting?" Serena asked caustically.

He shook his head seriously. "No, that was not interesting."

"You'd have done better in Paris, I'm telling you."

Donovan nodded. "Yeah, yeah, I know."

"Well, it is less likely you'd have been shot, that's for sure," Serena said, laughing. After a few moments of silence she asked, "So how's your girlfriend?"

Donovan glanced over at her, a surprised look on his face, then shook his head disdainfully. "I actually wouldn't know."

"And why is that?" Serena asked, surprised.

"I haven't seen her for about four days," Donovan said evenly.

"Is she nuts?"

He grinned. "No, just busy."

"Hmmm…" she said contemplatively. "Was she really pissed about me showing up at your house?"

Donovan waited a few moments to answer. "She wasn't thrilled about it, but I wouldn't say she was pissed. Maybe a little paranoid."

"About what?" Serena asked, already knowing the answer.

"About you wanting me back," Donovan answered easily.

"Now why would you think that was paranoid?" Serena asked him pointedly.

Donovan glanced at her again, his teal eyes showing surprise. "Because it's not true, is it?"

"Getting you back wouldn't be a bad thing for me," Serena said noncommittally.

Donovan shook his head. "And why in the hell would you want me back?"

"I'm not the one who broke it off, Pony, remember?"

"Yeah, but…"

"But what?" Serena said doggedly. "You're even better looking now than you were before, and I thought you were gorgeous then. You've always had the best personality out of all the men I've ever met. You're fantastic. What's not to want about you?"

"I think your memory is fonder than reality, babe," Donovan said, never really good at accepting compliments.

"I think you're wrong, babe."

They pulled up to a restaurant then, and the discussion ended there. They spent a nice hour talking about old times and other things. On the way back to the office, Serena looked him over again. He was wearing dark brown pants, a white shirt, black suede deck shoes, and the black suede jacket. He had a lot of style now.

"So how come you didn't dress like this when we were together?" she asked, grinning.

Donovan laughed. "I grew up. Everybody has to sometime."

"Yeah? So how come you grew up so gorgeous?"

"Is that what I did?" Donovan asked, giving her a sidelong glance.

Serena nodded. "I'd say that's a definite yes."

"Uh-huh…" Donovan looked unconvinced.

He dropped her off at her car a few minutes later and went back to the office. He was feeling tired, but he was determined to finish clearing his desk off. By the time he was done, he was surprised to note that it was almost five o'clock. He stood from his desk, stretching carefully—mindful of his shoulder, which was aching at that point—and reached over to pull on his jacket.

As Donovan approached his car he noted a familiar figure leaning against it. He felt irritation rise in him as he realized Jeanie was watching him closely as he approached. He was sure she already knew he'd had lunch with Serena, since Christian had seen them drive up together and Jeanie and Christian had become pretty good friends. He knew Joe's cousin wouldn't miss an opportunity to dig at him a little bit.

"To what do I owe this honor?" he asked, trying to keep the sarcasm out of his voice but not totally succeeding.

"Do I have to have a reason to drop by and see you?" Jeanie replied evenly, her eyes fixed on him.

Donovan looked at her for a long moment even as he unlocked the passenger door and held it open for her. She got in, glancing up at him as he closed the door.

"Where am I dropping you?" he asked once he'd gotten in, avoiding her last question.

Jeanie didn't answer for a long moment, surprised at his brisk manner. "Home, I guess," she said finally.

"So what's up, Jay?" he asked then, tiredly.

"Does something have to be up?" Jeanie all but snapped. "Last time I checked you were supposed to be my boyfriend."

Donovan laughed with dry humor. "Yeah, that's what I thought too." His teal eyes stared straight ahead.

"What's that mean?" Jeanie asked, narrowing her eyes at him.

"It means that if I was really your boyfriend you'd be around more often," Donovan replied, not in the mood to play games. His shoulder was aching wildly, and he felt totally exhausted. The last thing he wanted was to play word games with her.

"I told you I have the academy—you know how time-consuming it can be," she said, then gave him a pointed look. "I thought you were behind me on this."

"Yeah." Donovan nodded, his tone cool and even. "It looks like I'm way behind you."

"But Serena certainly isn't, is she?" Jeanie said, her eyes flashing.

Donovan nodded. "Oh, yeah, here we go…"

"What?" Jeanie replied defensively

"So how did Christian tell you so quick? What, did he call you out at the academy or did he just text you?"

"One of the other guys in your unit told me, as a matter of fact. But I was actually the one that called Christian. I wanted to check in with Midnight on my ride-along schedule, and he answered her phone. And he wasn't ratting you out, if that's what you think. He told me you were at the office today. I told him to transfer me to your line. One of the other guys picked up and said you went to lunch with some redhead. I figured the rest out for myself. It didn't take a genius."

"Okay," Donovan said, nonplussed by the fact that it hadn't been Christian who had told her. "Point is, I don't see you for almost a week, I have lunch with my ex-girlfriend, and suddenly it's imperative that you see me. Nice."

"What did she want?" Jeanie asked, ignoring his other statements.

"She wanted a quick lay in the back seat of my car," Donovan said. "What the hell do you think, Jay? She came to have lunch with me, big deal." He made a gesture of futility.

"Oh, yeah, I'll bet that was her only reason."

"What difference does it make? I have to want her back, don't I?" Donovan snapped, irritated at having to have this discussion with her. "I thought you knew me better than that, anyway."

"I do, it's her I don't trust."

"Well, why don't you just worry about me for the time being," Donovan said, trying to end the fight before it got out of hand.

Jeanie didn't reply, just shook her head. After a long silence she looked at him again. "So where are you headed?" she asked softly.

"I have physical therapy," Donovan replied, his tone short.

"I'll come by your house later," Jeanie said, her voice again subdued.

Donovan sighed. "If you just want to fight, Jay, don't bother."

"Hate it when they're difficult outside of the bedroom, huh?"

Donovan glanced at her, the look on his face showing his surprise. "That's not fair," he said finally. "I never treated you like that."

Jeanie looked back at him. They were in front of her house by that time. Finally she shook her head, blowing her breath out in a frustrated sigh. "You're right. I'm sorry. Look, I'll come over tonight and we'll talk, okay?"

"Fine," was his short reply. Jeanie got out of the car, and he drove away. She watched him turn the corner, then, shaking her head, she walked inside.

Later that night Jeanie let herself into Donovan's house. He'd given her a key and the security code after he'd been shot, wanting her to be able to get in without him having to tap in the code every time. "Donovan?" she called out. She noticed the light was on in his bedroom and headed toward the room. When she walked in she saw that he was lying on his bed, still fully clothed; he'd taken the time to kick off his shoes and take off his jacket. His right arm was draped over his eyes, and he was breathing evenly. She could tell he was asleep. It was only eight o'clock at night, and she wasn't sure why he was in bed so early.

"Donovan?" she said softly, touching his hand.

He stirred, then groaned as he lifted his arm away from his face.

"What's wrong?" Jeanie asked.

"Whoever made up the term *physical therapy* obviously never heard of the word *torture* first," Donovan said, sounding exhausted.

Jeanie sat down on the bed. "That bad, huh?"

"Bad enough." Donovan moved carefully to sit up. "So," he said, his tone changing, obviously ready to get down to the serious stuff.

"What's going on with us, Jay? What's going on with you?" He asked the second question looking into her eyes, sure he knew what was coming.

She didn't disappoint him. Jeanie was immediately hesitant, then shook her head slowly.

"Jay," he said, putting a finger under her chin to stop the movement of her head. "Don't try to tell me there's nothing wrong. There is, there has been since I was shot. You don't think I can feel it?"

"I…" she began, sounding unsure. "Donovan, I don't know what it is. But I feel like I gotta get out and breathe for a while. You know?" she said the last with a look that beseeched him to understand.

Donovan gazed at her for a long moment, then nodded slowly. Yes, he did know what she meant, only it was usually him that needed to get out to "breathe."

"So what are you saying, Jay?" he asked, knowing but wanting to hear it from her.

"I just need to back up for a while," she said, sounding unsure even as she did.

"Okay…" Donovan said solemnly, watching her eyes.

"I mean," Jeanie said, confidence gaining in her voice, "I still want to see you… but I think we need to see other people too. Things are just too much right now."

Donovan nodded. Jeanie didn't know if it was in agreement or if he was just humoring her. When he said nothing she continued. "The academy's more than I expected it to be, and with all the studying and the preparation for inspection and stuff, I just don't have

106

time for a relationship too. I want to be fair to you."

Donovan continued to watch her as she spoke, staring back into her eyes disconcertingly. He didn't say anything, but his face was a mask of cynicism.

"Say something," Jeanie said finally, when the silence between them stretched for too long.

"What can I say to all that?" Donovan asked calmly.

"You can tell me that you understand, or that you hate me, or something," Jeanie said, becoming frustrated by his complacency.

"I do understand, I don't hate you, and what else can I say?" Donovan replied, still just as calm.

"Damn it, Donovan. I'm not saying I never want to see you again. I mean, you're my first and everything… I still want to see you."

Donovan shook his head. "I don't work that way, Jay."

Jeanie looked shocked. "What do you mean? I can't see you?"

"I mean, I'm not going to date you like we've never been a couple," Donovan said evenly.

"Why not?"

"Because, Jay, you and I have gone way beyond that, and I don't go in reverse in a relationship."

"So it's all or nothing," Jeanie said, sounding angry.

Donovan didn't reply, just looked back at her.

"That's not fair, Donovan," she said, knowing she sounded like a child.

"I'm not the one making the rules here, Jay," Donovan whispered.

"But I don't want to lose you…"

"Then don't break up with me," Donovan said simply. There was no plea in his voice, but his eyes said differently.

"Donovan!" Jeanie exclaimed, feeling confused and for some reason angry. "How can you not want me to break up with you, but not be willing to see me if we do?"

"Look." Donovan put his hand gently on her leg, looking right into her eyes. "Some guys can gear back. Go back to something casual when the relationship doesn't work out. But I'm not like that, not with you, not this time."

"But—" Jeanie started. His lips on hers stopped her. He kissed her until she was breathless, holding her against him with his right arm. When their lips parted she was clutching the front of his shirt with both hands.

"I care a lot about you, Jay," Donovan said, his lips still very close to hers, still meeting her gaze. "But I don't share."

Jeanie looked back at him, finally understanding what he meant. She closed her eyes for a long moment, then nodded. "I get it," she said solemnly. "I just… I really need time right now." Her voice sounded a little stronger at the last.

Donovan nodded. "Okay," he whispered.

Jeanie stood up, loath to leave his arms but knowing she needed to now, before she chickened out. She walked out of his house feeling like she'd just lost her best friend, but knowing it was better than the strain they'd both been under in the last few weeks. She knew it was what they both needed, she just hoped she hadn't made a mistake doing this while Serena was in town to try and reclaim her hold on his heart.

Donovan stared off into space for a long time after Jeanie left, feeling a little sick. He told himself it was the painkillers he'd taken when he got home from physical therapy. Somewhere in his heart he knew that wasn't it, but he hadn't been willing to beg her to stay. Getting up from the bed, he went into his bathroom and took two more pills, then stripped off his clothes and climbed into bed to wait for them to knock him out. It was almost ecstasy when he couldn't think anymore, when the medicine made it to his veins and made him too tired to even move. He dropped off to sleep. For the next five days, he fell into the pattern of taking painkillers and sleeping, wanting to escape the thoughts that crowded in every time he was conscious for too long.

****

Christian and Susan didn't see each other for most of the week following their night and day together. Susan's classes had been cancelled due to a problem at the college. Randy's classes were of course cancelled also, so Susan and she spent the week alternating taking care of the children. It gave Susan far too much time to think about Christian. She wasn't sure what their night together meant. She wasn't foolish enough to think that suddenly Christian was in love with her; she was sure that wasn't the case. What concerned her the most was how he would act toward her now. The guilt had long since set in about cheating on Warren, and she knew she needed to tell him what had happened. Well, maybe not exactly what, but at least that she had slept with Christian. She didn't see the point in telling him that she'd stayed with Christian the entire day following their night together.

Every time Susan thought about what they had done she couldn't help the flutter that started in her. She wasn't sure if the sensation came from her heart or her libido. What she did know was that Christian had certainly made her feel a great deal more than Warren had ever come close to.

It was the following weekend when Susan decided she needed to talk to Christian about everything that was swirling in her head. On Saturday she waited until noon for him to come up to the house. When he didn't appear she checked in the garage for his black Jaguar; it was there. Finally she drew up the nerve to go down to his room. She knocked on the door and heard him groan something close to the "Come" he usually said. She peered into the room. He was lying on the bed, a sheet covering his lower half, his chest bare. He had one arm thrown over his eyes and the other resting on his stomach.

"Christian?" Susan said hesitantly, walking over to sit on the bed next to him.

He lifted his arm, peering at her with one light blue eye. "What?" he asked tiredly.

"Are you sick again?" she asked, worried immediately.

"No," he groaned, his voice almost a whisper. "It's called a hangover. I don't suppose you've ever had one."

"Well, no," Susan said, grinning. "But I would guess that the last thing you want to do right now is talk, right?"

"Very perceptive."

110

Susan nodded, standing up. "Is there anything I can do?"

"Yes." He reached out and pulled her down next to him. "Stay here with me," he whispered. The sound of his voice made her tremble.

Susan kicked off her shoes and sat back down, leaning against the headboard. Christian rested his head against her stomach, much like he had when he was sick weeks before. Susan slid one hand through his hair, smoothing it, and rested her other hand on his back. After a few minutes she felt his hands at her blouse. She looked down and saw that he was unbuttoning it and pulling it out of her slacks.

"What are you doing?" she asked, raising an eyebrow at him.

Christian didn't answer, but when her blouse was unbuttoned, he laid it open and snuggled down against her bare skin, kissing her softly as if in explanation. He fell asleep, and Susan sat watching him.

When he woke a few hours later, Susan had fallen asleep. He got up carefully and went into the bathroom. When he came back out, he walked over to the bed. He watched her sleep for a while, then couldn't resist the urge to touch her skin. Sitting down, he slid his hands over her stomach and up over her satin-and-lace bra. He bent his head, pressing his lips against her skin. Susan woke to the sensation of his hands and lips on her. Her hands moved to his hair, even as she sighed. Her response spurred him on, and within minutes they were making love. Afterward Christian lay on his stomach with his arm and leg thrown over her possessively.

"Can we talk now?" Susan said softly.

Christian lifted his head long enough to give her a critical look, then lowered it again, resting against her shoulder. "Why do women always want to talk?" he asked drily.

111

Susan smiled. "Because we like to understand what is happening."

Christian sighed deeply, snuggling a little closer. "Fine, talk."

"I do need your participation, you know."

"I'm listening," Christian said, grinning against her shoulder.

"Christian Collins, you know what I mean."

"God," Christian said, starting to sound irritated. He sat up. "What is it you need to understand?"

Susan was ever amazed at how good-looking he was. "I just need to know what this means." She gestured to their bodies, and her clothes lying on the floor.

Christian raised a jet black eyebrow. "You aren't looking for a proposal, are you?"

"Be serious," Susan said, rolling her eyes.

"Well, then what is it you're looking for?" Christian lay on his back and reached over to his nightstand for a cigarette.

"You aren't going to smoke…"

"As a matter of fact, I am," he said, lighting the cigarette and taking a long draw. He only smoked when he was tense or irritated. Being questioned by her was making him both.

Susan was silent for a long time, watching him smoke his cigarette. She knew he did it, but hadn't actually seen him do so very often. He never smoked in the house, because of the children. She sat up, pulling the sheet up to her demurely.

"What did you do before you came here?" she asked, curious about the "colorful past" she'd heard Joe refer to.

Christian looked at her for a long moment, wondering what she'd heard. Then he shrugged. "Lot of things."

"Like what?"

"Like running drugs…" Christian said, watching her closely for her reaction. Susan's eyes widened, but she said nothing. She nodded, wanting him to continue. Christian shrugged. "I worked for a drug dealer. I needed the money."

"Did you do drugs?" Susan asked, surprising herself with her directness.

Christian looked at her for a long moment then nodded, his eyes not leaving hers.

"You don't still," Susan said, shaking her head, not wanting to think that he did.

"No." Christian shook his head as if to back up the statement. "I only did it for about a year. Too expensive a habit."

"What drug did you do?" Susan asked, curious in spite of herself.

"Coke." Christian was still watching her, not sure how he wanted her to react.

"Cocaine?" Susan looked surprised, but not overly so. Christian nodded. "So where does Geneva Glasstone come in?" she asked, raising an eyebrow at him. She'd heard her mother talking to Joe about Geneva and Christian. Susan knew her from the parties she'd been to with her parents as a younger girl. She'd heard Geneva referred to as a man-eater, cradle robber, and the not so nice term of ball-breaker.

Christian's face indicated his surprise that she apparently knew about him and Geneva. He realized then that he shouldn't be surprised; her mother was aware of Geneva. It served to figure that she would have warned Susan off, citing his relationship with someone like Geneva as a good reason not to get involved with someone like him.

"What do you want to know about her?" he said, amused.

"She was your employer for a time, wasn't she?"

"Yes. She paid me to escort her to parties." Christian's light blue eyes glittered humorously.

"And to sleep with her?" Susan gave him a direct look, even as she cringed inwardly at her own boldness.

Christian laughed drily, then shook his head. "No, I slept with her all on my own," he said, giving her a wry grin.

"But why?" Susan thought he could have slept with the most beautiful women in London.

Christian shrugged. "She taught me a lot, and she was interesting in her own way."

"Okay…" Susan said, nodding slowly. "So why have you slept with me?"

Christian grinned, having wondered when she'd get around to this question. He reached over to put out his cigarette, and sat up to face her. Without a word he pulled her to him, kissing her again. He pulled the sheet she held to cover herself from her grasp, sliding his hands over her breasts, making her shudder. He lay back, pulling her over him and looking up at her. Still not speaking, he moved his lips to her neck, actually nipping at her skin with his teeth. The sensation made her gasp. He continued to her shoulder, then pulled back to look at her. Her deep blue eyes were fixed on his, then she lowered her head and mimicked his actions.

It excited her when he drew in a sharp breath, grasping at her back. She moved her lips back to his then, kissing him deeply and feeling his hands move over her skin. Within minutes they were both breathless again, and his hands on her waist guided her body down over his, his body sliding smoothly into hers. Susan gasped at the contact and began to move with his rhythm. Again she lowered her head to kiss his neck, biting his skin and feeling him shudder in response. As their movements became more frenzied, anticipating release, she felt him grasp her hips, guiding her down harder on him. Susan gasped as she climaxed. Her mouth was still pressed against his shoulder, and in reaction to her body's release she bit down into his skin. Christian, already beyond control and on the very edge of his own climax, jerked up in reaction, sent into shudders of excitement. Susan's eye tooth caught his shoulder when he moved so sharply, cutting into his skin.

When they both lay panting, Susan saw the blood on his shoulder. "Christian!" she exclaimed, aghast at having caused him injury.

Christian glanced down, and seeing the blood, shrugged. "S'okay," he said, grinning.

"But I hurt you…"

"What do you think sent me over?"

"You liked that?" she asked, looking at him curiously.

"I like a lot of things," Christian said, his tone low.

Susan looked shocked. "But pain?"

"You know what they say," Christian said. "There's a fine line

115

between pleasure and pain. Some of us just go a little farther over that line than others."

Susan stared at him, curious in spite of herself. "So, how far over that line have you gone?"

Christian looked contemplative. "Pretty far."

"Really?" Susan widened her eyes, looking very innocent at that moment.

"Yeah," he said, sliding his hand over her body and bringing it up to touch her face gently. "But that's not really my thing. And I wouldn't go there with someone like you."

"Why not?" Susan asked, still sounding very young.

"Because for one thing, I don't really like it all that much, and for another, I wouldn't want to mar this beautiful skin." He slid his other hand over her back, caressing her.

"But you've done things before…"

"I've done a lot."

"Doesn't this hurt?" she asked, indicating the cut on his shoulder.

"Some," he said, but looked unconcerned.

Susan bent her head, kissing the wound as she would a child's "boo-boo." Christian shivered at the contact. When she lifted her head, she saw that he was watching her. His eyes were trained on her mouth; his blood was on her lips. Without a word he put his hand to the back of her neck, guiding her lips down to his. His tongue slid along them, tasting his blood, and then he kissed her deeply. When their lips parted, Susan looked at him for a long moment.

Christian grinned. "Too dark for you?"

Susan gazed back at him, a pointed expression in her deep blue eyes. Then she lowered her head, and this time slid her tongue over the cut on his shoulder. He closed his eyes and breathed in deeply. Her lips moved to his then, and Christian was surprised when her tongue touched his. He responded excitedly, kissing her deeply. They spent the rest of the afternoon exploring each other's bodies and enjoying it thoroughly.

As the sun set, Christian caught Susan's quick glance at the clock. "What?" he asked, curling his body around hers.

"I, uh…"

"What?" Christian said as he looked down at her, his voice stronger now.

"I have something I have to do this evening," she said, averting her eyes from his.

"With him, right?"

"Christian…"

"Cancel it," he said, no-nonsense.

"I can't." Susan turned to look at him. "We're having dinner with his parents. I have to go, Christian."

He looked back at her, his eyes smoldering as they narrowed. "Alright, but after dinner's over, I want you back here with me." Again his voice held no room for argument.

"Okay." Susan nodded, already knowing there was going to be a problem. She hadn't seen Warren in a week, and she knew he'd expect her to go to his apartment with him.

Two hours later Susan sat in an elegant restaurant with the man that was supposed to be her fiancé and his parents. It felt strange to her as she looked at Warren over and over; he just seemed ordinary. The conversation was always the same, talking about the weather, school, and the latest gossip around the society set. Susan sat silently, watching them talk. Warren's parents were fairly attractive people, in a rich, groomed sort of way. His mother, Margaret, had brown hair, cut to hang just to her shoulders. Her makeup was very subdued, as was her beige dress. Warren's father wore a dark brown suit and a starched white shirt. Susan wondered if they ever added any color to their wardrobe. She realized suddenly that they didn't even seem to notice that she wasn't talking. They just continued the conversation without input from her; as long as she kept looking like she was listening and nodding her head every so often, no one noticed. *Is this what my life is going to be like?* she wondered idly.

"Susan, dear?" Margaret said, looking at her finally. Her voice was very cultured.

"Yes?" Susan said, coming back to the present.

"I asked what your plans were after graduation. Will you stay on at the Sinclair home?"

"Yes, I love the children."

"Well, just until we have our own, of course," Warren put in, taking her hand in his.

Susan looked at him for a long moment, then nodded. "Of course, I don't want children right away…" she said, trailing off as she saw Warren shake his head.

"Nonsense," he said. He looked at his mother then. "Susan loves children, she just doesn't want to make the Sinclairs angry by leaving too soon. But you have to realize, darling, that you have to live your life too."

Susan nodded. "Yes. You're right." She was thinking along very different lines than he was.

As she watched Warren continue a different discussion with his parents, she wondered what he'd say if he knew what she'd been doing hours before. She wondered how he'd react to being bitten on the shoulder, or if he'd tell her what to do to please him. The lovemaking they'd had was always quick and quiet. Warren wasn't an expressive lover; he basically went about it like a procedure. Susan always came away from the experience feeling like he thought he'd done her a favor. She tried to keep her mind off Christian. It was hard not to think of the possessive tone in his voice when he'd told her he wanted her back with him when dinner was over. The thought that he wanted her that much made her feel warm and excited.

When dinner was over, Warren and she bid his parents goodbye, and then Warren took her hand and led her to his car. He opened the door for her and then got in on the driver's side. Without asking her, he drove to his apartment. Susan hadn't been able to gather the nerve to tell him that she wanted to go home. He led her inside, then turned to her and kissed her ardently. Susan closed her eyes and tried to kiss him back. She knew she needed to try and feel something with him—he loved her, after all, and they were engaged. Forcing herself to relax, Susan allowed him to lead her to his bedroom, where he undressed her. She lay down on his bed and closed her eyes, wondering if he'd notice that she wasn't really into what they were doing.

She heard him undressing and opened her eyes to watch. Warren did have an athletic body, but it didn't have the strength that Christian's seemed to exude. Warren was very pale, especially compared to Christian.

Warren glanced up, seeing her staring at him, and looked surprised. She'd never watched him undress before; she'd always kept her eyes shut, waiting for him to come to her. He wondered at the change. When his clothes were off, he lay down next to her. He tentatively touched her breasts, and kissed her again. Again Susan closed her eyes, wondering if it would be very wrong to think about Christian while Warren made love to her. She knew thinking of Christian would excite her and maybe make her respond better to Warren. Aware it was a terrible thing to do, but desperate to spark some kind of fire between herself and her fiancé, she thought of the things she and Christian had done that afternoon. Before she knew it, she found herself responding to Warren's kiss with an ardent one of her own.

Warren was surprised at her sudden eagerness, but he didn't notice that her eyes were tightly closed. He moved over her, entering her tentatively. Susan had to hold back the laugh that wanted to bubble up from her throat. She realized then that no amount of imagination could endow Warren the way that Christian was blessed in this area. Susan learned the art of faking it that evening. She felt horrible for doing it, but she knew he'd just keep trying until she orgasmed or got irritated enough to tell him to stop.

As Warren drove her home afterward, Susan knew she shouldn't see Christian that evening. After Warren dropped her off, she went to her room. She undressed and sat on her bed for a long time. Finally, she gave up and put her pants and shirt on from that afternoon, then went down to his room. Without knocking, she walked in. He was asleep on the bed, lying on his stomach. Susan looked down at him, thinking how much more powerful his body looked than Warren's.

As if he sensed her presence, Christian turned over, looking at her and then at the clock pointedly. "You rich people must eat a lot."

"I…" Susan began, not sure what to say.

"You went with him, didn't you?" Christian said evenly.

"He hasn't seen me in over a week," Susan supplied weakly.

"Did you fuck him?"

"I, well, he—"

"It was a yes or no question, Zan. *Did you fuck him?*" His words were measured, his voice low and threatening.

"Yes," she said, staring back at him defiantly. "He is my fiancé, after all."

"Oh, yeah, like I could forget." Christian nodded. Then he pinned her with a look, his light blue eyes narrowing slightly. "Did he make you come?"

Susan didn't answer. She knew she shouldn't have come down to his room.

He reached up and pulled her down to the bed so her face was within inches of his. "Answer me," he said through clenched teeth.

"What if he did?"

"Did he?" Christian said, his voice a whisper now. "Did he make you come like I do?"

Susan's breath caught in her throat. She was surprised at her instant reaction to him.

"Did you think about me while you were fucking him?" he asked, his voice becoming huskier as his lips brushed hers. "Is that why you came? Was that it, Zan? You were thinking of me, huh?" He started to say more, but her lips stopped him. She hated the fact that he was right, and that his words were exciting her again.

He took off the clothes she'd just put back on, and he made love to her more aggressively than he ever had before. Afterward he lay next to her, breathing heavily. He put his lips next to her ear. "Don't ever leave my bed to go to his again," he said, his voice husky but very serious. Susan shivered at the intensity of it, and snuggled closer in his arms.

****

In the week that passed after Midnight's "procedure," things were extremely strained in the Debenshire home. Four days after the abortion Midnight got up early in the morning. Rick heard her in the shower and realized she was planning to go to the office. He knew it wasn't a good idea. She'd been restless for the last couple of days. But he also knew she was in pain, because he knew the way she moved, and although she'd been trying to hide it, it was obvious she was still hurting. He wanted to question her—he wanted to drag her to the hospital himself—but it would be impossible. He waited for her to emerge from the bathroom. He was dressed in jeans and a black cotton shirt, and he was just settling his shoulder rig when Midnight walked out.

She looked at him, her eyes narrowing slightly, but she'd guessed he wouldn't let her out of the house without him. She continued getting ready, and when she walked out of the bedroom he was there waiting for her. Rick said nothing as he opened the front door. He walked out to his Mustang and held the door for her, fully expecting her to be difficult. She surprised him by getting into the car without comment. He glanced over at her as he got in; Midnight stared straight ahead, her jaw set. Rick shook his head, feeling irritated at the coldness in her but knowing it would do him no good to try and talk to her.

He drove toward the office, reaching over to turn the radio up. Eventually he put Def Leppard's *Slang* into the CD player. Forwarding through the tracks, he settled on the song that had been going around in his head all night: "Where Does Love Go When It Dies?" He'd begun to worry that some of the words fit the situation he and Midnight were in currently. He sang along, glancing at her a few times and noting that she seemed to be listening.

When the track ended Rick turned the radio down, looking over at her. "Are we ever going to talk again?" he asked, obviously upset at the thought that they wouldn't.

Midnight looked at him for a long moment, then shook her head slowly. "I just don't want to get into this right now…"

"When, Midnight? When can we talk?" Rick asked, his voice holding the intensity that made him who he was.

"Rick…" Midnight said, looking away from him.

Rick held his hand up. "Okay." He didn't want to push her; he was afraid of what she'd say. They drove the rest of the way in silence. He walked her to her office and left her there. On his way out he ran into Christian coming in.

"Hey," Rick said, stopping the younger man. "Do me a favor, will ya?"

Christian nodded. "Sure."

"Keep an eye on Midnight for me," Rick said, his voice low.

"You got it." Christian put a hand on Rick's arm. "She okay?"

Rick looked pensive, then blew his breath out in a deep sigh and shook his head. "I don't know."

Christian was surprised by Rick's tone. He recognized the defeat in his voice, and it bothered him somehow.

Things seemed to be getting back on an even keel by the end of the week. Donovan hadn't reappeared at the office, but by that time everyone in "the family" knew he and Jeanie had broken up. Midnight was still working tirelessly to find Donovan's assailants. There'd been a few leads, but not too much to go on. The shooter and his friend seemed to have disappeared. Midnight brought Christian in on the team working on the case, but on an office basis only. She also kept it very quiet that he was working with her, aware that the more people that knew Christian was working with them, the more likely it was someone would try something on him.

As things turned out, it became more evident that Christian was at odds with "the family" than working with them, or so it seemed. When Rick stopped him in the parking lot one day after work, it was apparent to Christian right away that Rick had a serious bone to pick. He had no way of knowing, however, that Susan had accidentally slipped her and Christian's physical relationship into a conversation. She'd been expressing her confusion over how to see things and cited that being physically attracted to someone like Christian didn't automatically mean love, even if they'd made love. She'd stopped just short of saying "made love," but Rick had caught her meaning and stormed out of Midnight's office. Susan had had a half day at school and Christian had picked her up and brought her to the office. Midnight and Rick were to drive her home. When Rick strode up to him purposefully, Christian tensed, sure he knew what was on the older man's mind. He was right.

Without a word, Rick punched Christian in the face. Christian went down, but got to his feet quickly, warily watching the other man, his body tense. When Rick moved in for another blow, Christian was faster and moved out of his range just in time. Christian's hands hung at his sides, tense and ready to do battle, but he made no move to bring them up to actually strike at Rick. Susan and Midnight came running over, even as a group of off-duty officers gathered to watch the battle, one of whom was Frank Devereaux.

"Rick!" Midnight yelled, moving to get between the two men. She held her hands up, her back to Christian. "It's over," she said, her tone commanding.

"Like hell it is!" Rick snarled, moving to get around his wife.

"Stop, Rick, now!" Midnight yelled.

Susan had gone to Christian and was looking up at him. Christian was shaking his head, not looking at her, his eyes still on Rick. He was waiting to see if Rick would try another punch. He'd let him have the first one, since he knew what it was about and Rick was right in a way. But he certainly wasn't going to let the man hit him again. The first time had hurt enough. Christian had been pretty sure he never wanted to tangle with Rick Debenshire, but now he knew for sure.

Rick stood glaring at Christian over Midnight's head. Midnight had her hands on his chest and was slowing forcing him backward.

"If you ever touch her again..." Rick said.

Christian raised a jet-black eyebrow at the other man. "That's up to her, ain't it?" he said derisively.

Rick shook his head, starting forward again, but Midnight's surprising strength stopped him, as did her words. "Stop, *Lieutenant*, now!" The emphasis on his rank made it clear she wasn't his wife at the moment, but his chief. Rick looked at her, his deep blue eyes meeting hers and narrowing.

"Don't fucking do this, Night," he said, sounding hurt and angry at the same time.

Midnight shook her head, staring back into his eyes. "Don't make me."

After a few long moments, Rick broke away from her and stalked off. Midnight watched his retreating back for a long time, then turned to Christian. She walked over to him and touched the bruise already starting on his cheek.

"I'm sorry," she said softly.

Christian grinned. "Don't worry about it. I knew it was comin' eventually." He looked at Susan then, and Midnight knew they'd be having a discussion later. She didn't relish being in Susan's shoes at that point.

"I guess you had to tell him, right?" was Christian's first comment when Susan walked into his room that night.

Susan hesitated, not knowing what to say. "I… I didn't mean… I never meant to tell him."

Christian raised an eyebrow. "Interesting that he knows then, isn't it?"

"I told you I didn't *mean* to tell him, not that I didn't," Susan said stiffly, feeling very uncomfortable at having his biting sarcasm turned on her.

"End result was the same, wasn't it?" Christian fingered the bruise on his cheek, a disarming look in his light blue eyes.

"I know." Susan sat on the bed next to him. He was sitting up, his shirt open, his jean-clad legs stretched casually before him. Susan reached out to touch his cheek, still looking into his eyes. "I'm sorry."

"Not as sorry as I am," Christian replied stubbornly, his countenance darkening a bit. "There's two people I didn't want to tangle with here—Rick was the other one."

"Christian…" she began, taking on a pained look.

"Stop," he said, the beginnings of a grin on his lips.

Susan began to grin as well. "Tell me this," she said. "Why did you let him hit you?"

Christian looked back at her for a long moment, his lips twitching as if he was trying to decide what to tell her. Finally he shrugged. "'Cause he was right. I did sleep with you, and I didn't have a right to."

"That's not true. We both wanted it to happen, so it did."

"Is that what happened?" Christian raised an eyebrow. "I recall alcohol being involved."

"Not enough to make me senseless."

"I wasn't talking about you."

Susan looked back at him, her mouth hanging open for a moment. But then she started to shake her head. "Not last time—last time you were hungover, but nowhere near drunk." She narrowed her eyes at him for a moment. "You weren't drunk the first time either."

"Maybe your uncle doesn't have to know that…"

"Why are you trying to excuse me?"

"It's what you need, isn't it? An excuse? A reason?" Christian said, his voice low, his eyes veiled.

"Is that why you think I'm here?"

"Isn't it?"

"Christian, I don't need a reason to be with you. I just want to be with you." She reached out, touching his hand. "You make me feel so much. You challenge me, you make me respond… It's hard to explain."

Christian looked at her for a long moment, his light blue eyes narrowed as if looking for some sign of deception. "I think you should go," he said finally.

"Why?" Susan said, surprised at his change in mood.

"Because I don't need to give your uncle a reason to come after me again."

"He won't. Midnight will beat him senseless if he does."

"I don't need the protection of a woman," Christian said irritably.

"Christian, that's not what I meant. I just meant that you don't have to be concerned with my uncle." She said the last still touching his hand, her eyes firmly on his.

"Yeah, well I can handle him," Christian said, pulling his hand away. "Look, just go on back to the house now."

"Christian, I want to stay with you," Susan said, practically pleading.

"Why? You don't have to prove anything to me."

"I'm not trying to prove anything to you."

"What makes you think I want you here?" Christian said, his tone droll.

"Do you want me here?" Susan asked, her voice indicating her lack of confidence.

"No," he said. "I just want you." Without warning, he pulled her into his embrace, his lips covering hers instantly.

As usual, his kiss set off every sense in her body. Susan found herself gripping his shoulders and moving her body closer to his, sliding her hands down his chest. Within minutes their clothes were in a pile on the floor and his hands were making her writhe and grasp at him. Susan made a point of moving over him, trying to get a little ahead of him. She moved down his body, surprising him when her mouth hovered over him.

"Zan…" he said, his voice low, his breathing deep. He clutched at her, trying to pull her back up his body.

Susan looked up at him, her deep blue eyes dancing with the sense of power she had at that moment. She could sense his tension, and was enjoying the fact that she was causing it. She took him in her mouth then and felt him gasp, his hands burying themselves in her hair. Within a few minutes he was frantic in his need.

"Where the hell did you learn this?" he said, his voice strangled, and oddly irritated too. "Did you learn it from him?" His hands tensed as the thought settled on him. "Zan?" he said, his voice still

129

highly charged. After a few more moments, she moved to kiss his stomach, sliding her body seductively back up his. Christian groaned, guiding her up enough to be able to slide her back down on him. They both tensed as their bodies met and the fervor increased. They cried out in their release, and Christian's voice was right next to her ear. "You're mine, you got that? Mine."

Susan drew in a sharp breath at the possessiveness in his voice, and she clung to it, even as she clung to him in her orgasm.

They lay together afterward, Susan tracing her nails in a lazy pattern over his chest.

"So?" Christian said a few minutes later.

Susan lifted her head to look at him. "What?"

"Where'd you learn that?" he asked, deliberately calm.

"Why?" she asked, knowing what he thought.

Christian was silent for a long moment, then lowered his head to put his lips next to hers. "Because you better not have learned it from him." His voice was serious, and Susan didn't doubt for a moment that he was too.

"Why, would it bother you if I did?" she asked innocently.

Christian narrowed his eyes at her all the same. Then he shook his head. "I don't like the idea of you bein' that intimate with him."

"But it's okay to be that intimate with you?" Susan was starting to see the double-sided standards he was holding her to.

Christian didn't answer, just looked back at her as if to say, *Too late.*

"He is my fiancé, remember."

"Then what're you doin' with me?" Christian replied, his voice still low and husky.

Susan didn't answer this time. She wasn't sure what to say.

"That's what I thought." Christian sounded satisfied.

They were both silent for a while. She lay in his arms, her head on his chest, stroking the hair there. Christian caressed her hair, his other hand cushioning his head. It was a comfortable moment. *Odd, that*, Christian thought. He usually wasn't at ease in a woman's presence without having sex with her or with all of their clothes on. This was neither, and it still amazed him how content he felt with Susan lying with him. He refused to examine the feeling closely for fear that his survival instincts would kick in and force him to drive her away too. So he lay quietly, stroking her hair and feeling warm and comfortable.

It was Susan who broke the silence, but her voice was so soft and relaxed that even the questions she started to ask didn't antagonize him.

"What were you like when you were little?" she said, glancing up at him.

Christian was silent for a moment, then grinned. "Just about as big a pain in the ass as I am now, only younger."

"I don't believe it," Susan said, shaking her head. "I'll bet your mother loved the hell out of you."

Christian laughed lightly. "That she did. Spoiled me to death as well. Too much, actually. I didn't know it until I was older, but she'd spend a lot of her pay on special things for me and deny herself everything. I tried to make up for it when I was old enough to work." He sounded serious by the time he'd finished the statement, and Susan

131

lifted her head again to look at him.

"Christian, you can't fault her for doing all that for you. She loved you—that's why she did it."

"I know," he said, hugging her a little closer. "I just wish I'd been able to do more for her."

"You saved her life, didn't you?"

"Hardly. I made a couple of phone calls. It was Joe that saved her life."

"If you hadn't had the sense to call him... If you hadn't loved her enough to try anything to get the money you needed? Christian, you saved her life just as much as Joe's money did, if not more. You were the driving force behind making everything happen the way it did. If she hadn't had you, she would have died in that hospital, alone." Susan touched his cheek, wanting desperately to make him understand. He was a good man, even if he tried to make everyone think differently. Susan knew he'd been involved with some seedy things, but she also knew that it had all been done to keep things together for his mother as well as himself.

Christian looked at her for a long moment, narrowing his eyes but grinning at the same time. "Since when did you become my champion?"

"Since I got to know you better."

"Carnally?" he replied, his grin widening.

"Cad," she said, her grin as wide as his.

"Tramp," he shot back.

Susan lowered her head, kissing his chest and snuggling back against him. They fell asleep that way.

CHAPTER 4

Donovan rolled over, groaning as he heard the buzzer to his front door intercom. "What?" he muttered blearily.

"Pony?" Serena said hesitantly.

He hit the button for the front door locks. "Come in."

A couple of minutes later, Serena walked into his room. It was the middle of the afternoon on Saturday; she was surprised to find him still in bed.

She had no way of knowing he'd spent most of the week there. The night before he'd finally dragged himself out of bed long enough to eat and take a shower. He'd lain on the couch for a few hours, lazily flipping through the TV channels. Eventually he'd given up and crawled back into bed. It had been a long week, and he knew the weekend was bound to be worse. He was used to spending most of the weekend with Jeanie. They'd gone hiking, or skating, or just walking around the boardwalk in Mission Beach. Other times they'd spent the day watching movies or driving up to Julian to have lunch and walk around the small town looking in all the shops. This weekend would be so different that he didn't like the thought of facing it. That was why he had yet to crawl out of bed again.

"What're you doing here?" he asked, sitting up. He wore only sweatpants, since the weather had been unseasonably warm the last few days.

"I told you I'd come to see you," Serena said, her tone slightly chiding. She sat next to him, looking him over. "You look… different. Why?"

Donovan shook his head. "I'm fine. I've just been kind of reclusive this week."

"Okay…" Serena said, nodding, then pinned him with a look. "Why?"

"Jeanie and I broke up." He said it quickly, as if doing so would make it easier to take. Then he shrugged. "I guess I've just been bummed."

"She was dumb enough to let you break up with her?" Serena said disbelievingly.

Donovan laughed, the sound anything but humorous. "Yeah, even dumber, she broke up with me."

"Whoa…" Serena sat back, looking sincerely stunned. Then she grinned sympathetically. "That's gotta be a first for you."

Donovan looked speculative for a moment, then curled his lips in a sardonic grin. "As a matter of fact, it is."

"Well, she was nuts," Serena assured him. Donovan rolled his eyes cynically. "She was, Pony. You're a helluva catch, and if she didn't realize that, I'm certainly not going to clue her in." She crossed her arms over her chest, looking defiantly at him, a grin playing at her lips.

"I see," Donovan said, nodding slowly. "So you plan to take advantage of my weakened senses, is that it?"

"Precisely."

Serena succeeded in dragging from the house. They ended up driving out to the beach and walking along the shoreline. They talked about Paris, her job, her apartment there, how her brothers were doing, how her parents were doing. Then they talked about how Randy was, and how Darrell's business was going and who he was currently dating. Serena noticed that mention of anything pertaining to the department or his life seemed too sensitive, so she steered the conversation away from those subjects. She didn't really want to talk about his job anyway; it was all too weird for her to fathom. Trying to picture Donovan as a police officer was still impossible for her.

By the end of the day, Donovan was exhausted, and was easily talked into allowing Serena to cook dinner for him. He lay on the couch in his house, staring absently at the television, dozing off a couple of times.

Serena stood in his kitchen with a feeling of unrealism. That morning she had hoped to at least visit with him for a few hours. She'd never expected that they'd spend the day together, nor that she'd be cooking for him that evening. Her appraisal of his kitchen received extremely high marks; he had obviously maintained his culinary appetite. In fact, she was hesitant cooking for him—he'd actually been the better cook between the two of them. She didn't know if she'd quite measure up. When the food was done, she had to wake Donovan to tell him it was ready.

Donovan grinned absently to himself as he sat down.

"What?" Serena asked, seeing it.

He smiled. "I... I'm just not used to eating other people's cooking in my own house."

"I don't want to hear any criticism either, Mr. Curtis. Just remember that a chef is always more comfortable in his or her own kitchen."

Donovan raised an eyebrow at her as he took his first bite. Serena watched, not realizing she was holding her breath until he nodded, and she expelled it. But she did see something in his eyes other than approval. "What?"

"Nothing," Donovan said, continuing to eat.

"Pony…"

"Nothing, Rena."

"I know you have some critical comment to make, so make it and we can go on from there," Serena said, trying to hold down her irritation. She knew she was overreacting; Donovan had in no way indicated anything but approval for the food she'd prepared. It was just something she thought she'd seen in his teal eyes. When they'd been in school together it had taken him a while to venture criticizing her. He'd always tried to be supportive and helpful, but she'd always had a problem with criticism and he knew it. It had taken a number of failed exams and her sheer desperation to stay in the culinary academy to get him to finally give her the constructive criticism she needed to achieve better grades. And now she could feel that she'd failed again, but Donovan wasn't owning up to it.

"Rena," he said, shaking his head slowly, "I'm not the chef here. I have no place to criticize, nor will I." He sounded very serious, which told her that she needed to back off. They weren't on the same ground they'd been on years before. Serena took her cue from that, knowing that if she didn't back off, she could quite possibly end this fledgling reunion before it began.

136

Finally, she blew her breath out in a lusty sigh. "I'm sorry. I'm used to the head chef down my neck all the time... I'm sorry." She smiled at him, watching his eyes closely.

Donovan looked back at her for a long moment, then nodded, picking up his wine glass and taking a drink. He watched her over the rim. He remembered well her temper when it came to criticism. Nothing had changed in that arena. He remembered how tense she'd be for days after he'd made a constructive comment. He'd always carefully avoided any comment that could be construed as critical, unless he knew it would affect her grade or standing in their class. He wanted her to succeed because he knew she wanted to succeed, and therefore had been willing to withstand her sharp tongue and angry silence to help her do just that.

They were no longer classmates, and yet he still withheld his comments, because he didn't want to make an issue out of something that wasn't important.

Later that night, Donovan lay in bed thinking about the day. He had enjoyed Serena's company. She was far different from Jeanie. She was more serious about a lot of things, but he knew she still didn't approve of his career choice. He could see it in the way she refrained from discussing his job. He knew that part of it was probably prudence on her part, not wanting to bring up Jeanie or anything that might make him think or talk about her.

Of course, that thought led to thoughts of Jeanie. He knew their breakup was hitting him hard. He couldn't put his finger on just why. What he didn't want to think about was that she had come to mean more to him in the short time they'd been together than he'd realized. It actually hurt him a little bit to think about her now. The realization bothered him. He never wanted to be one of those guys that pined after a girl that had left him. He wondered mildly if it was only because she had broken it off. He fell asleep thinking along those lines.

Midnight was half asleep when she felt something dropped into her open hand. It was cold metal. Before she could wake up enough to see what it was, another object the same size was dropped to join the first. She closed her hand over them and sat up. She was wearing an over-sized Oxford shirt open to just above the curve of her breasts. Midnight rubbed her eyes with her left hand, her right still holding the hard metal objects. When she opened her eyes, she saw that Rick was standing next to the bed, giving her an angry look.

"What?" she asked, already irritated. She opened her hand and looked down. It was her wedding ring, and... his. "What is this?" she said, looking up at him again.

"It's what you want."

"Excuse me?" She looked at him like he was losing it.

Rick narrowed his eyes at her. "You obviously don't want that on your finger." He pointed to her ring. "Or the other on mine."

"Rick..." Midnight began, shaking her head.

"A divorce, Midnight," he said through clenched teeth, his eyes flashing angrily at what he thought was her purposeful obtuseness. "Is that what you want?"

"A what?" Midnight replied, suddenly very awake and very serious.

"You heard me." Rick's expression let her know he was serious as well. "I have to know, Midnight. I can't go on like this."

Midnight looked at him for a long moment, seeing for the first time the worry in his eyes. She suddenly saw the fear there and knew it was her fault.

"Jesus…" she breathed, shaking her head. "Rick, no. I mean, I don't want a divorce. I never wanted… Shit, I guess that was hard to know, wasn't it?" She grimaced as she looked back up at him, seeing it written on his face. Reaching out, she took his hand and pulled him down to sit on the bed next to her. Rick watched her, his expression guarded.

"I'm sorry," Midnight said, her tone softening. "I've been so busy feeling like shit, and feeling sorry for myself, I forgot you didn't know what was going on in my head. Jesus, babe." She reached out to touch his cheek. Rick closed his eyes at her touch, and Midnight knew she'd been hideously unfair. "I love you. I never stopped loving you, Rick. I just hated… I hated what I had to do. It hurt me, and I guess in a way I wanted to hurt you for it."

"Midnight, don't you think it hurt me? Christ, that was my baby too. How do you think it felt having to make that decision?"

"It didn't look that hard, from where I was sitting," Midnight said honestly.

"It was hard, Midnight."

"Rick," she said, her eyes taking on a pained look. "It was so hard having to sign those papers, to tell them…" She hesitated, drawing a deep breath and looking away from him. "To tell them to kill my child."

"It was our child," he reminded her gently.

"Yes, but it didn't seem like that. It seemed like… like I was alone."

"You made it that way. You shut me out. Hell, you even went to the clinic to keep me away."

Midnight nodded, as if accepting what he was saying. "I just wanted it done. I wanted it over, so I could go on with my life…" She shook her head, her voice trailing off.

"A life without me?" Rick asked, still not reassured that it wasn't ultimately what she wanted.

"No!" Midnight said vehemently. She looked down at the rings in her hand again, shaking her head. "I've lost some weight, and my ring was so loose, I took it off to get it sized."

"All I could think about was last time…" Rick trailed off. Midnight knew he was talking about five years before, when she'd sent the ring to him in England. It had been a horrible time for them, and Midnight knew it had taken its toll on both of them.

"Rick, I never wanted a divorce." She looked directly into his eyes then. "I love you. I never stopped."

Rick looked at her for a long moment. Then, blowing out his pent-up breath, he reached for her, pulling her to him. Midnight leaned against him, feeling him relax as he crushed her against him. "I love you, Night. The thought that… that you hated me, that you wanted to leave—it was killing me."

"I know, babe, I know," Midnight said, crying suddenly. The tone in his voice was so lost, so pained, it hurt her almost physically to hear it. "We'll get through this together. I'm sorry that I didn't see what I was doing to you. I was so busy feeling sorry for myself. I'm sorry."

They embraced for a long time, holding each other but not speaking.

When Midnight moved back, she looked up at him. She could see that he was feeling much better now. She made a point of putting his wedding ring back on his left ring finger. Then she gave him a pointed look. "And I expect it to stay there, Mr. Debenshire."

Rick grinned, looking at her through the veil of his light brown curly bangs. "And you, *Mrs.* Debenshire, better get that ring sized and back on your finger fast as well."

"Count on it."

"I am."

Later that night, they lay in bed with Midnight curled up in Rick's arms, her head resting against the hollow of his shoulder. He stroked her arm absently with his thumb as he nuzzled her hair and kissed her temple. "Babe, are we going to talk about it?" he asked softly. He was worried about making her angry, but he also knew she needed to let out some of the feelings she'd been harboring over the last couple of weeks.

Midnight nodded, quiet for a few moments. "It's hard. I mean, not like last time, 'cause last time I really didn't have a choice..." She trailed off. "I mean, Dickerson really didn't give me a choice." Rick nodded, his eyes narrowing at the mention of the man's name. Dickerson had brutalized Midnight, throwing her against a wall and causing the miscarriage that had almost cost her life. "But this time," Midnight said, her voice almost a whisper, "this time I had to actually do it. I had to go in there and tell them I wanted to terminate a pregnancy." She glanced up at him, her eyes glossy with tears. "It was the hardest thing I've ever had to do in my life."

"I know, babe," Rick said softly. "That's why I was hoping I could share it with you, try to cushion the pain... something..."

"But I wouldn't let you," Midnight said, finishing his sentence. "It was like I had to feel it, Rick. I had to feel it all. I let the pain wash over, almost drowning me, like I deserved it somehow."

Rick hugged her tighter. "No, babe. Jesus." He put his finger under her chin, turning her face up to his. "Midnight, you were saving your life. You were saving… me."

"You?" Midnight said, blinking.

"God, yes, Night. If you'd gone through with the pregnancy, and if something had happened to you, I couldn't have gone on." He shook his head mournfully. "I love you too much, you are everything to me. You're like the air in my lungs—without you I'm dead. Don't you think that it hurt me, knowing that by telling you to have an abortion I was killing my child, because I wanted you to live?"

"I never thought about it like that," Midnight said, shaking her head. "God, Rick, that must have been so hard. I wish… I should've… I should've been here, there…" She trailed off, knowing she hadn't been. She'd been wallowing in her own sorrow, her own pain. "Rick, I'm sorry," she said again, feeling desolate.

"Night, it was both of us. It was the whole thing." Rick knew now that being the people they were made it inevitable that their own stubbornness had caused the rift, and the subsequent isolation during the situation.

Again they were silent for a while. It was Rick that broke the quiet this time, his concern for her overriding his desire not to irritate her.

"Night," he began cautiously. "You're still hurting, aren't you?"

Midnight glanced up at him, knowing it was a waste of time trying to lie to him. Finally, she nodded.

142

"Have you talked to your doctor? Is that normal?"

"No, and I don't know," Midnight said softly.

"Well, you will, and then you'll know."

Again Midnight glanced at him, her grin sly. Then she nodded, garnering a sigh of pent-up breath from Rick. He'd been worried she was going to argue with him, but he realized she wanted to keep the peace they'd established as much as he did.

****

In the following weeks Donovan saw more and more of Serena. Eventually it became almost like old times. There was still the distance about his job, and the fact that she was still jealous of his natural cooking ability, even though she tried to hide it. Donovan had almost forgotten what he suspected was her resentment of his ability to make anything good. When they'd been together, there had been comments and looks, but Donovan never said anything to her about it. After they'd broken up, he'd realized how much tension there had been, and how relieved he'd been when it was over. This time they weren't competing for grades, so the tension wasn't near what it had been, but he still noticed it.

They went out a few times, even went drinking together. Donovan hadn't even bothered trying to take her to 10-7, knowing she'd hate it instantly, and part of him would always remember his and Jeanie's first time there. He didn't want to go there with another girl. One night they ended up at a dance club in Pacific Beach. Donovan was stunned when he went to the bar to get a drink and saw Jeanie.

He felt his insides tighten as she walked over to a man she was evidently with. Donovan's mouth dropped when as he saw Christian turn to talk to her.

Jeanie walked back over to Christian, still amazed that she had actually managed to drag him to a dance club. She wasn't nearly as surprised a few minutes later.

"You shit!" she said to him, hitting him in the chest with her balled-up fist, laughing all the while.

"Hey!" Christian said, laughing too. "I never said I hadn't been here before. You just thought I hadn't."

"No wonder the bartender winked at you when we came in." Jeanie narrowed her eyes at him. "You've slept with her, haven't you?"

"Maybe," Christian said, sitting back in his chair. He surveyed the room, his gaze coming to rest on a pair of teal-colored eyes watching him closely. "Uh-oh," he said, mildly chagrined.

"What?" Jeanie asked, following his line of sight. "Oh…" She'd seen Donovan just as he turned to walk away from the bar. She looked back at Christian. "I didn't know he'd be here," she said apologetically. "I didn't know he even came to this place. He usually goes to 10-7."

"Maybe that's why he's here." Christian nodded toward another part of the club.

Jeanie turned around and easily located Donovan again, his height and fair hair setting him above most of the crowd. She also easily pinpointed who he was with, her long red hair drawing her attention instantly. Jeanie's eyes narrowed dangerously, and not even seeing the look on her face, Christian could sense her tension immediately. He shook his head, picking up his shot of tequila and knocking it back, then reached over and touched her gently on the shoulder. Jeanie jumped and turned to look at him.

"Don't get spun up, Jay, it won't do no good," Christian said calmly.

"I'm fine." She picked up the shot she'd ordered for herself, ignoring the fact that it was the drink Donovan had introduced her to, the particularly lethal Stars at Night. She knocked it back, feeling it burn all the way down. She got up and headed to the bar, ordering another one from the blond bartender. As she waited for the woman to make the drink, she said, "So you know Blue, huh?" For some reason she wanted the woman to know that she and Christian were only friends.

"What?" Tara asked, and then said, "Oh, you mean London?"

"London?"

"That's what I call him." Tara shrugged, laughing. "'Blue' sounded too much like one of my daughter's cartoon characters."

Jeanie laughed at that, nodding. "Yeah, I guess you're right."

"You with him?" There was no jealousy in Tara's voice, or her expression.

Jeanie smiled. "He's a friend."

Tara leaned in conspiratorially. "Let me tell you somethin'. If you get a chance to sleep with the guy, grab it. He's worth the time."

Jeanie widened her eyes at the other woman, but then started to laugh, shaking her head. She had always suspected Christian was probably good in bed, but having some woman she didn't know tell her to grab a chance to sleep with him was too unreal. Walking back to the table, she was still laughing.

"What?" Christian asked, giving her a wary look.

"Nothing," she said, grinning wisely.

"Yeah, right." Christian sounded wholly unconvinced. He glanced behind her, and his expression changed totally. "Uh…"

Jeanie sensed his presence moments before the scent of Tommy cologne reached her. She tensed again, refusing to turn around until Christian's light blue eyes settled back on her, as if saying, *Okay, now what?*

Jeanie turned around, irritated by the fact that she had to crane her neck to look up at Donovan. She smiled brightly. "Hi, Donovan, how's it going?" she asked, her tone almost too upbeat.

Donovan looked back at her for a long moment, then nodded. "Okay."

"How's the shoulder?" she asked, her voice still forcibly cheerful.

"Okay," he repeated, still not smiling. His tone was even—to his credit, Christian thought. Donovan didn't even look mad.

"Donovan," Christian said, nodding to the other man.

"Blue," Donovan replied, nodding in return. "I just thought I'd come over and say hello. I'd better get back."

"Yeah, don't want Serena to get lonely," Jeanie heard herself say, wanting to kick herself almost immediately. Donovan gave her a sharp look but said nothing in return. He turned and walked away, and Jeanie watched him go. After a while she saw Serena dragging him out onto the small dance floor; it was a slow song.

Christian sat silently, waiting to see how Jeanie would react. He knew it bugged her to see Donovan with his old fiancée. Jeanie had told him about Serena and how defensive Donovan had been about his old girlfriend—*Fiancée*, Christian corrected himself. He'd even been surprised by that. Although less so when Jeanie told him it was Donovan who had broken off the engagement. Randy's little brother seemed to have a definite commitment problem where women were concerned. Not that Christian was interested in anything remotely resembling a relationship. But Donovan was supposed to be the straight-laced, upstanding one. Christian also knew Jeanie had done the breaking up this time, and he suspected it had a lot to do with a general distrust for men and a lack of commitment on her part.

Watching Jeanie at that moment, Christian knew she was seething. When she turned to look at him she saw that he was watching her.

"What?" she asked automatically.

"Jealous?" Christian replied evenly.

"No," Jeanie said, too quickly. "I just thought he'd avoid getting tangled up with her again." She shrugged, trying to look unaffected.

Christian nodded, not bothering to look like he believed her.

"Do you dance, Blue?" she asked after a few minutes.

"Not if I can help it," he said, taking a drink of his beer and setting the bottle on the table. Just in time, since she grabbed his hand and pulled him out of his chair.

"Well, you can't help it," she said, grinning and pulling him toward the dance floor.

"Jay…" he started, knowing exactly what she was doing and not sure he wanted to be part of it.

"Just come on," Jeanie said, laughing as they got to the dance floor. "I won't hurt ya, I promise."

Christian pulled a face. "No?"

Jeanie laughed again as they moved together. She was surprised to find that he was actually a pretty good dancer. Without thinking too much about it, she moved closer to him, resting her head against the hollow of his shoulder. She inhaled the scent of Havana cologne, so different from the clean, sporty scent Donovan wore. Havana was kind of spicy and sexy, a lot like Christian seemed to be. Jeanie thought about what the woman at the bar had said. She contemplated the idea of actually going to bed with Christian. In spite of herself, she knew she was curious about how things would be with him. How he would kiss, what he'd do to arouse her.

Without realizing it, she'd closed her eyes, swaying with the music and feeling Christian's strong warmth supporting her.

"You're not gonna pass out on me, are ya?" Christian said, his lips right next to her ear so he could be heard over the music. His accent was still very strong.

"No." She lifted her head to look at him and was surprised to find his face so close to hers. He still didn't pull away when she looked up at him. Their faces were so close, and she'd just been thinking about how he would kiss. Jeanie hesitated a second longer, then pressed her lips to his. It was as if he'd been expecting her to do it. His lips pressed back against hers, parting them to kiss her deeper. His hand moved to the back of her neck, caressing it and keeping her lips on his.

Jeanie was shocked to find herself responding to him. Her arms

148

were around his neck, her hands buried in his black hair. She felt very warm, and pressed closer to him, which only excited her more.

Christian had known they would end up kissing the minute she grabbed his hand to drag him to the dance floor. He also knew it was going to be her move, not his. When their lips did meet, he found himself wanting to make her respond to him. He knew it was some misplaced jealousy of Donovan's place in her heart, but he didn't care at that point. Christian was very aware of the fact that Donovan stood not too far way, and he could almost feel the man's eyes burning into him. It was a dangerous game Jeanie and he were playing, and Christian half expected Donovan to walk over and punch him out for kissing the girl.

When their lips parted Jeanie didn't look at him. She rested her head against him again. Christian could sense the turmoil in her; he could feel the nervous movement of her thumbnail on the collar of his shirt. He didn't know exactly what she was thinking, but he was sure she was trying to make sense of what they were doing.

A couple of hours at the bar, with the tension between Jeanie and Donovan and between Donovan and Christian becoming almost tangible, and Christian couldn't take it any longer. He stood up from the table and walked outside. Jeanie found him twenty minutes leaning with his back against the wall next to the side door. He was smoking a cigarette, and she noted two butts on the ground next to his booted foot.

"What's up?" she asked, leaning against the wall next to him.

Christian glanced down at her through the veil of smoke. "Not much for tension," he said simply.

Jeanie grimaced, then looked up at him apologetically. "I'm

sorry, Blue. I know I'm kinda putting you in the middle here..."

Christian looked at her for a long moment, then dropped his head back against the wall, staring up at the clear night sky. "S'alright," he said, his tone light. "Guess I'm just curious 'bout what comes next."

Jeanie was silent for a long moment, then took the cigarette from his hand and turned to face him, pressing against him suggestively. "Why don't you take me home," she said softly, staring up into his eyes.

"Yours or mine?" he asked, looking at her pointedly.

"Yours."

Christian nodded slowly, then pushing off the wall, he took her hand and led her to his car.

The drive to Joe and Randy's took only minutes. Neither of them spoke. The radio was on, and Matchbox 20's "3AM" was playing. Jeanie listened to it, almost laughing at some of the lines that seemed to fit her so well right now.

When they arrived, Christian led her to his room in the carriage house. Once inside, they looked at each other for a long moment.

"You sure about this?" Christian asked softly. He knew full well what they were there to do, but felt like he was taking advantage of her. She was his friend, after all.

"Did you ask the bartender that before you had sex with her?"

"No," Christian said. "But she wasn't my friend before we had sex. You are."

Jeanie nodded, understanding what he meant and comforted by the fact that it mattered to him. She wouldn't be a notch on his belt—

that was important to her. Without a word, she closed the small distance between them, reaching up to touch his cheek and then draw his head down to hers. She kissed him then, and felt his hands close around her waist as he pulled her to him.

They kissed for a long time, and it became apparent that he only planned to ask her once about being sure. Jeanie threw caution to the wind, giving herself over to the excitement coursing through her. She knew this wasn't true love; she knew it had nothing to do with caring or a relationship. It was carnal, and lust, and for once she gave in to it. She was sure she could trust Christian with this kind of abandon without fear of major repercussions. She was single, he was single. They liked each other. He was gorgeous and one hell of a good kisser!

She unbuttoned his shirt and slid her hands inside. He tugged her silk blouse from the waistband of her jeans and slid his hands up her bare back to her bra, unhooking it deftly. Jeanie gasped as his hands slid around to the front of her body, his thumbs stroking her nipples, sending shivers of excitement down her body.

After a few minutes, he lifted her in his arms and carried her over to his bed, still kissing her. A few minutes later his body was sliding into hers. She gripped his shoulders, surprised at how different it felt with him. His movements were just as expert as Donovan's had been, but they were more aggressive. The fact that she was still feeling the buzz of the shots she'd drunk at the bar made things different too. She'd never been very buzzed when she was with Donovan, not even the first time after the wine she'd had. Not like this. Christian was indeed different, but it felt good with him too. Jeanie wondered at that. Did it always feel good, or had she just gotten lucky? She'd heard enough of her friends complain about their men to know she'd probably gotten lucky with both guys. She stopped thinking as her body responded to the pressure of his, the sensations of his lips against her neck, and the way his body felt in hers.

Afterward the questions came back. Christian had moved to lie next to her on his side. He had his face buried in a pillow as he tried to catch his breath. Then he propped his head up, his elbow on that same pillow. He was looking down at her, a half-grin on his face. He could almost see her mind churning.

"What's goin' on in that head of yours?" he asked.

Jeanie looked at him, a grin tugging at her lips. "Actually, I was wondering how I managed to get lucky twice."

"Huh?" he replied, his jet black brows furrowing.

"Well, in my limited sexual experience, I've slept with a total of two men now. You know that. Anyway, I think I've been pretty lucky that both men were really good where it counts." She grinned roguishly then, her brown eyes twinkling.

"I see," Christian said, holding back his grin. "So I measure up, do I?"

"Measure up?" Jeanie rolled her eyes, knowing that he thought of Donovan as the proverbial Golden Boy. "Stop it," she said, poking him in the chest.

Christian just laughed. Then he gave her a serious look, raising a mocking brow. "So tell me again why we're here…"

"You didn't seem to mind a few minutes ago."

"I still don't." Christian grinned and trailed his finger along her jawline. "But I want to hear why you think we're here."

"Because of Donovan," Jeanie said, shrugging as if it didn't matter.

"Uh-huh. To get back at him for being with his ex."

"That's why I'm here," she said, narrowing her eyes at him suspiciously. "But why are you?"

Christian pursed his lips, looking into her eyes for a long moment. "Guess you won't buy that it's for purely physical reasons, will you?"

"With you? Normally," Jeanie said, smiling. "But that's not it, is it?" Her eyes searched his. "Why are you here, Blue?"

"Honestly?"

"Yeah."

He dropped his head back on the pillow, looking up at the ceiling, and let out a frustrated sigh. "To put a little distance between me and Susan," he said simply.

Jeanie's eyes widened as she moved to look down at him. "You and Susan?"

"Yeah…" he said, looking at her again.

"Wow." She shook her head as if she couldn't picture it. In truth, she couldn't. "So how come you need some distance?" she asked, wanting to understand his motivations.

Christian shrugged, shaking his head as if to deny what he was about to say. "We've been getting too close. She's different, and it bugs me."

"Different for you?"

"Yeah." Christian could see she was waiting for more of an explanation. "I don't treat her like I treat most women I sleep with. I don't even want to treat her like that. I usually keep a cool distance with women, but all I want is to keep her close to me. It's weird."

"What about me? You don't seem distant now… or does that come later?" Jeanie didn't sound jealous or angry; she was just curious about what he meant by "distance."

"It's different with friends, like you, like Tara. I hang around because there's a friendship there too. Unless, of course, the 'friend' starts expecting a relationship or something. But Tara doesn't expect romance or love and all that crap. But with Susan… I want to stay near her, I want to touch her, hold her, all the stuff I don't do with women after sex." He shook his head, then gave her a direct look and grinned. "Do I sound like a total asshole to you now?"

Jeanie shook her head, smiling. "I pretty much knew how you were before this," she said, indicating the bed and the two of them. Then she gave him a pointed look. "Are you in love with her, Blue?"

Christian blew his breath out, giving her a look that indicated she'd just lost her mind. "I don't believe in love, Jay. Never have, never will."

Jeanie shrugged. "Don't know what to tell ya, Blue. Sounds pretty serious."

Christian shook his head, as if she still wasn't getting it. "Hence the distance," he said, gesturing to her naked body.

She grinned. "Oh." They were silent for a while, lying together companionably.

"And how do you feel about this, now that you've done it?" Christian asked finally.

Jeanie was still silent for a few moments, then glanced over at him. "I don't know. Does it matter?"

Christian shrugged. "Can't be undone now," he said reasonably.

"No... So I guess I don't have to know how I feel about it."

"It really bugged you, seeing him with her though, didn't it?" he said, his tone sympathetic.

"Yeah... I just... I thought he wasn't like that. You know, moving from one relationship to another that quickly or easily."

"You did the breaking up, remember?" Christian pointed out calmly.

"I know, but what's that got to do with it?" she said, feeling angry for some reason.

"Is it what he wanted?" Christian asked carefully, sensing her irritation.

"He didn't stop it," Jeanie practically snapped.

"Could he have?" Christian shot back, knowing the answer.

"Maybe. He could have been willing to see me, at least."

"What did he say? That he didn't want to see you?"

"He said he wouldn't date me, that our relationship had gone way past that and that he wasn't willing to backtrack."

Christian nodded, giving her a pointed look. "Sounds reasonable to me."

"Well, thanks! You're on his side?" Jeanie sat up to look down at him.

"What did you want, Jay? You wanted him to go back to bein' a date?" He gave her a sly look, then started to nod. "You got scared, didn't you?"

Jeanie looked startled. "What?"

155

"Don't 'what' me." Christian sat up, staring at her with a knowing look. "Things were getting too close for you, so you bailed. But you weren't willing to let go of him all the way." He pinned her with a look then. "And you're pissed that he wouldn't play your game, aren't you?"

"Fuck you," Jeanie said, her eyes flashing angrily as she looked away from him.

Christian put his finger under her chin, turning her face back to his, his light blue eyes staring straight into her soul. "You just did."

Jeanie made a startled sound in the back of her throat, but then closed her eyes slowly. She was allowing what he'd said about her being scared to sink in—she knew he was right.

"Blue…" she began apologetically.

"Hey," he said, grinning. "I knew what this was about." Then he gave her a serious look. "I just wanted to make sure you did too."

Jeanie nodded, leaning her head against his shoulder. He stroked her back. After a few minutes he lay back, pulling her down with him. She lay half over him, so it was easy to lift her head to look down at him.

"I used you," she said simply.

"And I you."

Jeanie grinned. "Okay."

"Yeah," Christian said softly, kissing her lightly on the lips.

They fell asleep together a while later. Christian heard his door open, but he didn't bother to look up. He knew it was Susan—he could almost sense her shock. He heard the door close quietly and only then did he turn over. He'd been lying on his stomach with his arm around Jeanie's waist. It was very obvious that they were both naked. Christian knew Susan had seen it, and had known that they'd slept together. It was what he'd thought he wanted. But lying there in the darkness, he felt like the world's biggest asshole. The thought dragged at him. It pissed him off no end that he wasn't reacting to Susan even close to the way he thought he should be. She was too damn different, and to him that was dangerous.

Donovan was silent on the drive home from the bar. Serena knew things had suddenly become precarious between them. Donovan had just about dropped to the floor when he saw Jeanie kiss Christian. Serena had sensed his tension immediately, and knew he was still attached to his ex-girlfriend. She had no idea. Donovan hadn't been happy to see Jeanie with Christian to begin with, but then when Serena had dragged him to the dance floor and Jeanie had responded by doing the same with Christian, Donovan knew he was about to have a fight. He had watched them dance, and he'd seen the inevitable kiss between them. His blood had boiled at that; he'd had the strongest desire to hit Christian, but he could also see that it wasn't Christian initiating the whole thing. He had caught the Englishman's none-too-pleased look as Jeanie dragged him to the floor. Donovan had the distinct feeling that Christian was being used, and that Jeanie was doing it just to make a point. Because of that assumption, Donovan had held back the urge to charge the other man. He had simply watched, keeping his face calm and unperturbed.

Donovan had also noted that Christian had spent the rest of the evening looking coolly displeased about the situation. He'd seen the other man walk out of the bar. A few minutes later he had started to follow him, but then he'd seen Jeanie get up and follow Christian too.

Donovan hadn't been able to keep himself from going after them, and because the door Jeanie went through didn't close all the way and was located at the back of the bar where the music was much more muted, he could hear their conversation. When she'd told Christian to take her "home," Donovan leaned his head against the cool metal of the door, hoping silently that she meant hers. A moment later he'd had his answer. Without thinking he'd spun around, striding back to the bar and ordering a double shot of Cuervo Gold tequila. He spent another hour getting fairly drunk. Serena had taken his keys and was driving his car now.

Donovan rooted around in his CD collection, choosing Matchbox 20's *Yourself or Someone Like You.* He forwarded through the tracks and listened idly until "Back 2 Good" came on. He turned the song up and listened intently to the words. It described just how he'd felt at the bar, and the way his thoughts were swirling about him now.

He knew that he and Jeanie had gone past the breakup now, and she'd moved on. It was driving him crazy that she'd apparently moved on to Christian; he knew Christian was very likely to hurt her, if she got her heart involved with him. It bothered Donovan further that he cared if she got hurt or not. Once at his house, he went to the front door, punching in his security code automatically and walking inside. Without waiting to see if Serena was following him or not, he headed toward his bedroom.

He took off his jacket and threw it on the chair. He pulled his holster out of the back of his pants and tossed it on his dresser, then unclipped his badge from the side of his belt and threw that down too. Sitting down on the bed, he unlaced his Doc Martens and kicked them aside, then pulled his shirt tails out of his pants, unbuttoned his shirt, and lay down. He closed his eyes, feeling the world spinning just a bit. He knew he was too drunk, that it wasn't a buzz anymore, and that he needed to eat something to waylay the hangover he was due for, but he couldn't gather the energy to get up and get something.

"Pony?" Serena said, gently sitting down next to him.

"What?" he answered, without opening his eyes.

She touched his chest carefully. "Are you alright?"

Donovan stiffened noticeably. "I'm fine," he said, his teeth almost clenched.

"Pony…" Serena said, frustrated now, "You're upset about seeing Jeanie with that man, aren't you?"

Donovan didn't answer. He simply turned over on his side, his back to her.

"Pony," Serena repeated, almost angrily now. "I know you still have a thing for her, but don't you see how you're wasting your time?"

"Rena…" Donovan began, his voice holding a note of warning, but Serena ignored it.

"No, Pony, I'm not going to be silent this time. I'm sick of watching you pine for someone that obviously doesn't feel the same. And now she's in some other man's bed, isn't she?"

Donovan sat up, his anger and frustration driving him there. Grabbing her by the shoulders, he narrowed his eyes at her. "Shut up, Rena."

"Why? So she can kick you around some more?" Serena said softly, searching his face. She knew he was drunk, and she knew she was taking a big chance, but she took a deep breath and plunged ahead. "I love you, Pony. I always have. I just want to make you happy, and you know it's what you want too."

Donovan stared at her for a long moment, his eyes guarded. "Don't say that," he said, his tone warning again.

"It's true," Serena said, defiant now.

Donovan narrowed his eyes, feeling another rush of anger. After a long moment he threw himself backward on the bed. "Rena, just go home," he said, sounding tired suddenly.

Serena looked at him for a long time, then moved to lie over him, looking down at his face. "I don't want to go home, Pony," she said in a deep whisper. Donovan opened his eyes in response to her weight over him. "I want you to make love to me," she said then, staring down into his eyes.

They hadn't made love since they'd been "together" again. Serena had been more than willing, but Donovan had held back. He knew he was being ridiculous, but somehow it was like if he didn't sleep with Serena, it made them being together not an actual relationship. That Jeanie couldn't say he hadn't waited around long before jumping into bed with someone else. Of course, now Jeanie had done just that, Donovan was sure of it. Christian didn't strike him as the type of man to decline an offer such as Jeanie had made that evening. Certainly since he and Christian didn't exactly see eye to eye on most things. No, Donovan knew beyond a shadow of a doubt that Jeanie was in Christian's bed that night. *So why am I waiting?* he asked himself wryly.

With that thought gnawing at him, he looked back at Serena. His teal eyes almost burned with the barely contained anger and betrayal he felt. Serena knew exactly what was about to happen between

160

them; she knew it was basically going to be, as her older brother would put it, a "revenge fuck," but she didn't care. She felt his muscles tense beneath her, then he shifted her off him, moving to put her beneath him as he brought his mouth down on hers. Serena met his kisses with eager ones of her own. For now she'd accept his anger, and the sex it brought with it, but next time he'd make love to her.

Later that night, Serena lay curled up next to Donovan, asleep. Donovan, on the other hand, was fully awake and sober. He stared up at the ceiling, trying to push aside the thoughts of Jeanie with Christian. He tried to think about other things, but he didn't really succeed, eventually falling into an uneasy sleep just before three in the morning.

CHAPTER 5

Two weeks after the night in the bar, Jeanie went on her first ride-along break from the academy. At Midnight's request, she was allowed to split her time between ride-alongs and working on the case, which seemed to have grown cold in terms of new leads. Things were coming to light all the time. Donovan and Christian had rooted out a number of discrepancies in the inventory. So many things were missing. Mostly money, but sometimes drugs, firearms, and the like. Donovan had delved into researching the vehicles in the department's inventory the week before, having felt the need to take on the daunting task. By the following week, he was fully entrenched. Midnight sent Jeanie to help him, having no idea that the two were at odds. When Jeanie showed up in the basement offices where the vehicle files were kept, she was on edge. Donovan looked up as she walked in; his eyes showed surprise, but he said nothing.

"Midnight said to help you with the vehicle files," Jeanie said evenly.

Donovan said nothing for a long moment, then shrugged, mindful of his still sore shoulder. "Okay," he said simply.

To Jeanie's surprise and Donovan's credit, he was completely professional, too much so. By the end of the day, Jeanie was even more on edge. Giving in to her urge to try and settle something between them, she caught up to him in the department parking lot. He was halfway to his car when she reached him.

"Donovan, wait up!" Jeanie said, slightly out of breath.

Donovan turned to look at her, his face composed in a cool mask. "Yes?" he said, his tone polite—too polite.

Jeanie looked back at him for a long moment, wondering if she'd been too impulsive in chasing after him. "I was hoping we could talk..." she said cautiously.

"About what?"

"Donovan..." Jeanie said chidingly, but her voice held a note of the tension she felt.

"Fine," Donovan said, walking back toward the gates of the parking lot. Half a block away was a coffee shop; he headed for that. Inside, the shop had all the earmarks of the latest trendy coffee houses. There was jazz playing in the background and the tables were wicker and glass. The chairs were maple ladderbacks.

After ordering, they sat down. Donovan regarded her expectantly. "So, what's up, Jeanie?" he asked, pointedly using her full name instead of his nickname for her.

Jeanie hesitated, once again wondering what had possessed her to think he was going to be willing to talk. She also wondered if she'd overestimated his distress about her absence in his life, and the distance between them now. Finally, she decided that she needed to know, one way or another.

"You know," she began, giving him a patient if slightly irritated look, "we were friends before we were a couple."

Donovan looked back at her for a long moment, as if considering the thought. Finally he nodded, but said nothing.

"So why can't we be friends again now?" she asked plaintively.

Donovan's eyebrows creased as he gave her a look that said, *As if you didn't know.* After a moment he shook his head, blowing his breath out. "Too much has happened between us since then, Jeanie."

"Like sleeping together?" Jeanie put in sharply.

"For starters, yes," Donovan said, his teal eyes staring back into hers, his lips pressed together in a serious line.

"I see. Once you fuck 'em, you can't be friends with them anymore, huh?" Jeanie snapped, her eyes flashing angrily.

Again Donovan took his time answering, his face irritatingly passive. His voice was soft when he did respond. "I'd like to think there was more to our relationship than fucking."

Jeanie drew in a sharp breath at the hurt in his voice. "That's not what I meant."

Donovan looked back at her, his expression telling her that he didn't necessarily believe her.

"Donovan…" she said, reaching out to touch his hand. She was half surprised that he didn't yank it away from her. Instead he looked at her hand on his, as if he didn't recognize it. "Please," she continued beseechingly. "I didn't come here to fight with you."

"Fine," Donovan said. "Why did we come here?"

Jeanie shrugged. "I just thought we could talk, maybe smooth some things over."

"Like what?" Donovan asked, quirking his eyebrow at her. "Like you sleeping with Blue, or Perkins or Juarez?"

Jeanie looked shocked, then shook her head. "I didn't know… I mean…" She didn't finish the sentence, because Donovan had started to grin wryly.

164

"Yeah, well," he said, leaning back in his chair and stretching his legs out in front of him, looking at her disdainfully. Then he shook his head again. "Jay, if you want discretion about who you're sleeping with, don't sleep with other cops."

Jeanie immediately looked contrite. "I haven't slept with John Juarez," she said irritably.

"Does he know that?" Donovan replied coolly.

"Of course he does!" Jeanie snapped, then sighed as she looked at him. "What you're saying is that it doesn't matter, that everyone will think I have anyway, right?"

Donovan inclined his head. "It may be a big department, but news travels fast around here."

Jeanie nodded, not sure what to say, deciding that she didn't want to discuss other guys with him. That wasn't why she'd wanted to talk. "Okay, but what about us?" she asked, leaning forward.

"What about us, Jay?" he asked with a sigh in his voice, as if to say, *We covered this already.*

"Can we at least get past the strangers point again?" she said, suddenly desperate for someone she trusted to talk to.

Donovan looked contemplative, then to her dismay shook his head slowly. "Not right now. Things are still too raw."

"You're talking about the bar a couple of weeks ago."

"I'm talking about how I feel about you sleeping with Blue, yeah."

"Why does Blue matter more than someone else?"

Donovan didn't answer for a long minute, then shook his head. "I don't know, maybe 'cause I was worried about you getting hurt."

"But not with Perkins or Juarez?" she put in, confusion obvious on her face.

"I guess now I just don't care," he said evenly. He held his teal-eyed stare for a moment, but then looked away from her.

Jeanie was stung. She realized that in some way she wanted to know that he still cared about her, and by his admission he'd put an end to that hope. Suddenly all she could think about was getting out of the room. She didn't want to sit there with him anymore, knowing the way he felt. She knew now that trying to talk to him had been a mistake. Christian's words came back to her again. *You're pissed that he wouldn't play your game...* She knew that was exactly what it was, but she couldn't tell him that, not now, when he was looking at her so impassively. As if she didn't matter to him...

"I have to go," she said, abruptly standing up.

If Donovan was surprised by her sudden need to be somewhere else, he didn't show it. He merely stood too, nodding, his face a calm mask.

On the drive home, Donovan reflected on the conversation. He didn't understand why she didn't get it. Why she thought they could just be friends. *Because I love you too damned much, that's why*, he thought wryly. That's what he wanted to tell her, but he knew he couldn't, that she wouldn't want to hear it. She wanted everything to be simple and uncomplicated. He knew Jeanie didn't like heavy emotions, or complicated relationships that required a lot of effort and time put into making them work. It was Donovan's thinking that she was too young to be able to handle the commitment that a real relationship took. He knew all about that; he'd been there. With Serena.

In his heart of hearts, he knew that was why he'd broken it off

166

with her the first time. Her aversion to his attending the police academy, which was something he truly wanted to do, was a convenient excuse to break up. Now, years later, he knew he'd done the right thing. He and Serena were just too different. But he and Jeanie hadn't been. *Of course, I'm not the one that did the breaking up, am I?* Someone with the same commitment phobia had done it this time. It smarted, and the last thing he wanted to do was to hang around and be her friend while she dated every guy in the department.

The days that followed their conversation didn't fare much better. He kept a cool distance and she tried to understand, or at least cope. One week after their conversation at the café they ended up together in his car. Midnight had contacted her liaison at the Department of Motor Vehicles and Donovan was tasked with going through DMV's records to match up the department's ledgers.

After ten minutes in the car, Jeanie glanced over at him. His jaw was set in a line that she knew meant he didn't want to talk, but she decided to ignore that.

"So tell me again, what is it we're doing?"

Donovan glanced over at her, then looked back out at the road ahead of them. "We're going to go through DMV's records of what vehicles they say we own, and compare them to the current inventory."

"And where the records don't match?"

"That's when we start hunting. VINs have a way of turning up in the strangest places."

"Ah, yes." Jeanie nodded. "VINs are rather hard to dispose of, aren't they?"

They were talking about the Vehicle Identification Numbers given to every vehicle manufactured. The number was virtually impossible to obliterate, and they were recorded by anyone buying, selling, registering, or ticketing a vehicle.

After a long day, Donovan dropped Jeanie back at the office. She got out of the car without a word, but she wanted to say something. The entire day, he'd been polite and civilized, but by no means friendly. She missed their friendly banter, the discussions they'd had about everything ranging from music to food to politics. They had a lot in common, though differed in opinions on some issues, but she even liked the way he argued.

Shortly after their conversation at the café, she'd broken it off with John Juarez. She didn't like the idea that he was probably telling everyone that he and she had slept together, and considering he was an instructor at the academy in Cultural Awareness, she didn't need any rumors flying. John had been displeased about her discontinuing the relationship, but she told him she just thought it was better if they kept things on a professional level. As it was, she had slept with Tom Perkins. It was more or less a one-night-stand type of thing, and she regretted it ten minutes after it was over. Tom had come nowhere near Donovan or even Christian in the sex department, and she felt even farther from what she'd had with Donovan now. Especially since Donovan knew about it. Things were all mixed up, and she couldn't figure out how to make it right again.

Jeanie knew she couldn't blame Donovan for his attitude; she knew how her behavior must look to him. She looked like she'd lost her virginity with him and then gone on to sample every guy that came along. She talked to Christian about it that night. They'd gone to the bar again, and Jeanie was relieved and disappointed at the same time that Donovan wasn't there. After a few drinks they'd gone back to Christian's room at Joe's house. To their mutual surprise they didn't have sex, but instead lay on his bed, talking for the next few hours. They talked about Donovan, and about Susan. Jeanie was still struggling to understand what was happening to her, and why she continued to think about Donovan when things were so obviously over between them.

"So what am I supposed to do?" she asked Christian, rolling over on her stomach and propping herself up on her elbow to look down at him.

Christian shook his head. "You need to face up to the fact that he may think it's over, and he may even want it to be over, but you still care about him. That's the problem, babe," he said calmly.

"That's what you think?" Jeanie asked, narrowing her eyes at him.

"That's what I know."

She raised a cynical brow. "And how did you become so omnipotent?"

"When you slept with me, how did you feel?" he asked, his tone indicating he didn't expect her to lie to him.

All the same, she was slow in answering. "Guilty," she said finally, sighing.

"And when you slept with the other guy?" There was no hint of any jealousy or reproach in the question.

"Worse," Jeanie replied, flopping to her back and sighing again.

Christian moved to lean on his elbow over her. "You still care about Donovan."

"So how come he doesn't still care about me?" she asked, without addressing his statement.

"How do you know he doesn't?" Christian countered.

"He told me he doesn't," Jeanie said, in a way that challenged him to argue the statement.

He surprised her by doing just that. "Yeah? And what would you say if he'd slept with two or three other girls and wanted to know why you weren't jealous?"

Jeanie pursed her lips, narrowing her eyes at him. "Okay, so maybe I'd lie and say I hated his guts too."

"Alright then."

"Okay," Jeanie said, rising up to meet him face to face. "So what are you going to do about Susan?"

It was Christian's turn to narrow his eyes. "What's that got to do with what we were just talking about?"

Jeanie grinned. "You care about her, I know you do."

"Maybe, but it doesn't really matter."

"And how's that?"

Christian rolled his eyes at her. "For one thing, she's engaged, and for another, I don't do emotional bullshit."

"Why the hell not?" Jeanie asked indignantly.

"Jay…" Christian began, but she cut him off with a knowing nod.

"Yeah, yeah, I know, you 'don't believe in love and all that crap,'" she said, imitating his accent fairly well as she repeated his favorite statement about love.

Christian grinned. "Very good." Then he raised a jet black eyebrow, looking at her with a twist to his lips. "Now, remind me again why we're not having sex right now, instead of talking about all this crap?"

Jeanie shook her head, looking at him like he was a recalcitrant student. Reaching out, she tapped him on the forehead with her index finger. "Because we're friends and we do that better than sex."

"I don't think I'd go that far," Christian said, with the usual glint of humor in his eyes.

Jeanie just laughed in reply. They continued to talk and joke until she went home at 11:00. Trying to fall asleep that evening was difficult; his words kept coming back to her. What if Donovan really did still care about her? How was she supposed to know? Should she try to talk to him again? Her mind and ego gave her a resounding "NO!" to that thought. She knew she couldn't withstand him telling her again that he didn't care. Eventually she realized she'd just have to wait and see what happened. She just hoped things hadn't been irreparably damaged between them. The thought that he was dating Serena, his ex-fiancée, who could easily become his current fiancée again just as easily, continued to nag at her.

Things between Christian and Susan had become and remained tense since the night Susan walked in on him in bed with Jeanie. On the days he had to drive her to school, she pointedly read or stared out the window, ignoring him. Christian maintained an air of cool amusement, but he felt his anger rise when she made a point of telling him on a number of days that he didn't need to pick her up, that Warren would drive her home. Christian knew she was telling him so he would know she was going to his apartment after school. He tried not to be irritated by it, but found it impossible not to be. In his usual manner, however, he said nothing. But even Susan could sense his anger.

Christian spent many evenings putting the final touches on the inventory program he'd written for the department. He worked late into the night most days. He was at his computer one evening when Susan and Warren arrived home late. It was a Friday night, so Randy was off from school and had given Susan the evening off. Christian was sitting in the extra bedroom next to Susan's, which had been turned into a makeshift office. He heard them walk down the hall, and then talking in her bedroom. It became obvious to Christian that they were making out. He could also hear Susan telling him they shouldn't do this here. Christian agreed wholeheartedly; it was the last thing he wanted to hear.

It became increasingly obvious that Warren fully intended to make love to her in her room, whether she really wanted to or not. Christian was damned if he was going to stay out of their business.

Warren was lying over Susan on her bed when Christian pushed the door open. He could hear Susan's whispered protest, but Warren was obviously ignoring her words, or he thought they were just lip service. Her blouse was open at the front, his hand sliding over her skin up toward her breasts, when Christian cleared his throat pointedly.

Warren raised his head, turning it to look at Christian. He narrowed his eyes at the Englishman. "What do you want?"

Christian's light blue eyes bored into the other man for a long moment before he answered. "What I want," he drawled, "is for you to get the fuck off her, before I have to remove you." His voice was calm, but his eyes indicated that he meant it.

"Why don't you just turn around and leave, man. You have no business here. We are engaged, you know." He said the last giving Christian a smug look, sliding his hand possessively over Susan's skin again.

Christian's eyes flicked to Susan. She was watching him, her eyes wide. He could tell she didn't want him to cause trouble. Christian shook his head slowly, his eyes locked with hers, as if telling her she shouldn't be there.

"Are you going to leave?" Warren said. "Or do I have to make you?"

Christian gave him an almost gleeful smile as he straightened from the door frame he'd been leaning on. He dropped his hands to his side, gesturing with his fingers. "Oh, please, come here and try to make me."

Warren moved off the bed, taking the time to straighten his clothing. Christian stood watching, refusing to be baited into getting angry. He calmly waited for the other man to try something.

"Warren…" Susan said.

"Don't worry, Susan," Warren said, cocksure. "I'll get back to you soon enough."

"Don't count on it," Christian said. Then he looked at Susan, his eyes traveling over her still-exposed breasts. "But I'll take over where he left off, if you'd like."

It was a taunt, a nasty one, and he knew it would work; he wanted it to because he was itching to beat the living hell out of the

173

other man. And it did work, like a charm. Warren sucked in his breath in outrage and launched himself at Christian, ducking his head to try and catch him in the mid-section. It was a classic wrestling move, but Christian wasn't exactly the fight fair and by set rules kind of guy. At the last moment he raised his knee, catching Warren in the face, and brought his forearm down on the back of the other man's neck. The fight was over before it started. Warren lay on the floor coughing, and Christian leaned against the doorframe again, looking at Susan.

"Next time you're going to have guests over, love," he said, cool and calm, "tell them to mind their manners." With that, he turned and left the room.

Predictably, Susan appeared in his room later that night, full of anger and outrage. Christian told her to come in, but didn't bother to pull the covers up over his bare chest. He noted with satisfaction that her eyes were drawn to it and lingered over him as she walked toward him. She stood above him, hands on her hips imperiously.

"What is it you want, love?" he asked, his voice irritatingly smooth.

"You know full well what I want," she said. Christian grinned, staring back into her eyes suggestively. "You know what I mean, Christian Joseph Collins!"

Christian strove to hold back the wider grin that threatened to overtake the one already on his face. He hadn't realized she'd learned his middle name—it meant that she had been curious enough to ask around. Joe was the only one likely to know it, and Susan didn't usually question Joe about things like that. It amused him no end.

"Yes, love, I know what you mean," Christian said, his voice low.

174

"I want you to apologize."

"I'm sorry," Christian said dutifully.

"Not to me, you cad!" Susan snapped. "I meant apologize to Warren."

Christian shook his head. "Not bloody likely."

"You hurt him."

"And…"

"And you should apologize," Susan said, suddenly sounding like his mother.

"Did he apologize to you?" Christian asked pointedly.

"There was no, I mean, he didn't need to…" Susan stammered, her cheeks flushing with color. Although it was hard to see in the dimly lit room, Christian sensed it and found it necessary to increase it.

"So you doin' him regularly now?" he asked, pulling her down on the bed next to him as he sat up to face her.

"Excuse me?"

"You heard me," Christian said. "I want to know if you're doin' Warren on a regular basis now."

Susan just stared back at him openmouthed for a long moment, then shook her head. "That's none of your business," she said, embarrassed. She turned her eyes away from him.

Christian brought his hand up, cupping her chin not so gently and turning her back to face him. "Answer me," he said quietly, his eyes boring into hers. Susan remembered graphically the last time he'd said that to her. It had been the night she'd gone to dinner with

Warren and his parents, and then slept with Warren. Christian had asked her if Warren had made her come; she didn't answer and he'd said the same words to her as he had now.

"Yes, I've made love to my fiancé," she replied finally, trying to ignore the heat she felt starting deep inside her.

"Is he up to speed yet?"

"What?" Susan asked, looking unsettled suddenly.

He moved closer to her, his lips within inches of hers, making her catch her breath. "Does he make you feel like I do, Zan?"

"I—" she began, but his lips on hers stopped her. His kiss was deep, and it made her shiver from head to toe. He pulled her into his arms, drawing her across his body to lean against his legs. When their lips parted he looked down at her. They were both breathing heavily.

"I want you, Zan, now," he said, his voice deep with the heat between them.

"Yes... yes..." Susan said, knowing she was falling into the easy trap of his arms again. She knew she didn't belong there, and that there was no security in them, but she couldn't resist.

Later, as they lay in each other's arms, he slid his hands over her back, feeling warm and sated again. Christian knew that she was an addiction he needed to break, but he simply didn't want to just then. Her body was like a drug to him; he craved it, especially the closer she was to him. At the moment, she was still as close as she could get. His body was still inside hers, her head resting against his chest. He could feel her breath warm on his skin. It pleased him to no end that she had cried out his name over and over in her release. It was as if she was stressing over and over who she was with, who excited her that much. He knew it was stupid to think like that, but for some reason

176

the idea of her with Warren irritated him immensely. He fell asleep holding her close to him and thinking he shouldn't be so dependent on the feeling of her against him.

****

Jerry McCaffery sat looking out at the bay, watching one of the Navy's aircraft carriers maneuver its way out of the docking area. He thought briefly of his one-time dream to be a Navy pilot. The Navy wouldn't even let him anywhere near the aviation program; they said he was too short and his test scores were far too low for something as top notch as an aviator. They had told him he could become a recruiter someday, citing his slick used-car salesman look and attitude. Jerry had reeled at that. He thought he was pretty cool then—he thought he could be a Top Gun pilot like Tom Cruise in that movie. He considered himself a badass motherfucker; that's what he told himself in the mirror most mornings. His hair had been longer then, just past his collar. His brown eyes weren't really shifty, were they?

Sitting watching the aircraft carrier move along, he came back to the present. He had something going on that day, and he needed to concentrate on the matter at hand. Midnight Chevalier hadn't taken to the warning they'd sent when they put the hit on Donovan Curtis. In fact, the sonofabitch had actually managed to shoot one of the guys. If McCaffery had been thinking about it clearly, he would have admired Donovan for avoiding death and almost managing to take out one of his own attackers, but Jerry wasn't thinking clearly. Maybe if Curtis had died, Chevalier would have backed off, but now she had Curtis and that little slut Franco digging into DMV records he'd personally seen to disorganizing. It had been easy enough to gain access to the records, since he was IA. He'd simply gone into the folders and switched stuff around, obliterating some VINs and shuffling paperwork. DMV never really dealt with this stuff unless there was an inquiry, so they didn't look into the specific folders too often. They had the handwritten records and that's what they used. But now Donovan Curtis, in his infinitely thorough manner, was digging. It would only be a matter of time before he started checking access records. He'd find out that McCaffery had been in the records room for two full days right around the time the discrepancies with vehicles became obvious. They needed to derail Curtis, now.

"How's it goin'?" said a smooth voice to his left. McCaffery turned to look at the short Mexican kid sitting there.

"It sucks, that's the problem," he said. He motioned to the other man to sit down. They were at Seaport Village, and Jerry was sitting on the stone wall that ran along the back of the tourist trap. He figured nobody from the department would be around, especially on a gray day like this. Hardly any tourists had ventured out, considering the chill in the air and the dark skies.

Emilio Benitez sat down, glancing at the cop. The guy always looked nervous. He knew McCaffery was about to put the squeeze on him, but Emilio didn't really care. He just wanted to see Tiny Ako fired and brought up on charges. McCaffery was his way to get to the huge Samoan. Tiny and Emilio had met up recently at a house in South San Diego. Tiny had been on an entry team for a raid, and Emilio had been running the crack house they were working. Emilio had always thought himself a damn tough *cholo*, but he'd made the mistake of pulling a knife on Tiny Ako. Tiny's long reach and massive arms had given him the advantage over the shorter man. He could have drawn his weapon and killed Emilio on the spot. He would have been justified in doing it, considering the fact that Emilio had told him he was dead meat and would soon be *carnitas* for his pit bull. Instead, Tiny had lashed out with a meaty fist, knocking Emilio down. Unfortunately for Emilio, he was stubborn and stupid; he held fast to the knife and started to get up. Tiny grabbed him up and slammed him against the nearest wall in an attempt to dislodge the knife. Emilio had continued to resist, reacting to the humiliation Tiny was inflicting rather than the pain. It had finally come down to Tiny breaking the smaller man's wrist to dislodge the knife. Emilio had begun screaming "Police brutality" right away.

It was Jerry McCaffery who had been assigned to investigate Emilio's allegation. Midnight had initiated the investigation, knowing that Tiny was more than likely justified but also making sure she treated all of her officers equally. Tiny had understood, explaining to Midnight that the man had pulled a knife. Midnight believed it; Jerry McCaffery believed it, but he knew this was a good chance to get rid of Tiny Ako. He was still disgruntled over Tiny's "attack" on him regarding his comment about Jessica, Tiny's wife. The scene still played over and over in Jerry's mind, and every time Jerry imagined getting a chance to get back at the big Samoan. Now he had it, but there was something he wanted Emilio to do in the meantime.

"So," Emilio said impatiently, since McCaffery wasn't talking. "Whaddya want, man?"

Jerry looked at the Mexican for another long moment, using silence as a way to set him on edge; it worked almost every time. At least on people like Emilio. It never worked on Chevalier or Sinclair, which pissed Jerry off no end. He waited until the Mexican kid started to squirm noticeably, then nodded slowly.

"Need ya to do me a favor, Milio," Jerry said, as if he were just about to ask the kid to wash his car or something.

Emilio narrowed his eyes. "Yeah? What?"

"Hey, now." Jerry held up his hands in protest. "If you don't wanna do it, it's fine with me."

"Yeah, and if I don't, what happens?" Emilio knew McCaffery was as dirty as they came.

"Well," Jerry said, fingering the button of his sports coat, then looking out over the bay again. "Not a whole lot. I mean, other than a knife that was entered into evidence by one Tiny Ako will magically reappear just in time to clear that particular officer." Jerry looked at Emilio then, his face cool. "That would probably put a pretty big dent in that civil suit you got goin', wouldn't it? What're you suin' for? Two mill, right?" Jerry nodded, as if to himself. "Yeah, that'd be a damn shame, 'cause I know you got big plans for that money…" He let his voice trail off as Emilio started to nod.

"Yeah, I fuckin' knew there was gonna be a squeeze here. So what do ya want me to do?"

"I need your help in causing a little accident," Jerry said, steepling his fingers together.

"What kind of accident?" Emilio wondered how much Jerry McCaffery thought he could do without getting caught, or maybe he didn't care. "You want me to ice someone, don't you?" Emilio knew the answer before he saw the affirmation in Jerry's eyes. "Shit, man, that's like murder. I could go away for a long fuckin' time for that. I ain't inta all that shit."

"Yeah, well, you don't have to actually kill someone, just cause an accident at just the right place. With some luck, it'll kill the bitch."

180

Jerry spat the last out, feeling his usual anger and resentment well up as he thought of "those people."

Emilio thought about it for a long moment, then nodded. "Okay, what do I hafta do?" he asked, resigned to doing whatever it would take to get his hands on that two million dollars and get Tiny Ako fired.

Jerry stood up and indicated Emilio should do the same. Emilio followed him down the planked walk, nodding as Jerry explained the plan.

Jerry drove out of the parking lot at Seaport Village feeling very satisfied. He didn't like having to be the one to put the hit on Randy Curtis, but Devereaux had taken care of the other Curtis job. Hopefully this one would be more successful.

Things between Randy and Joe had been unusually strained since Donovan's shooting. Randy knew Joe was still angry about her comment about Midnight's brother, and that he didn't understand why she'd said it. In reflection, she knew it had been a stupid thing to say, and that it wasn't something he would easily forgive. She had made many attempts to make it up to him, all of which Joe had received with quiet reserve. One early evening about a month and a half after Donovan's shooting, Randy showed up at Joe's office. It was supposed to be her evening at school, but she had asked one of her classmates to take notes for her and had spent the last few hours at home getting herself beautiful for her husband. Joe looked up from his desk when she opened the door, and stared at her dumbfounded. She was wearing a teal silk blouse, with tailored black chinos and a fitted waistcoat. Her long golden hair was pulled back softly from her face and held with a black clip. She'd taken care with her makeup, enhancing her deep blue-green eyes and making her whole face seem to glow.

"Wow," Joe said, his handsome face breaking into a genuine smile. "What's the occasion?" he asked, his accent clear.

Randy walked into his office, shutting the door behind her and smiling at him. She went around his desk to sit on the edge, facing him. Joe pushed his chair back and, with one arm, slid her over to stand in front of him. He put his arms around her waist and looked up at her.

"The occasion is," Randy said softly, cupping his chin, her thumb stroking the slight stubble there, "that I'm madly in love with my husband, and I'm very sorry about being a bitch."

A slight grin tugged at Joe's lips, and he stood up. His body was very close to hers. His dirty blond hair fell forward over his shoulders as he looked down at her. "I know you were worried about Donovan," he said, his voice as soft as hers.

"Yes, but that was no excuse to strike out at Midnight. I know that hurts you, and I shouldn't do it."

Joe didn't answer this time, just watched her eyes.

"I love you," Randy said, so sincerely, searching his face.

Joe grinned. "I know that. And I love you. Things have just been... hard lately, ya know?"

"Yes, I know." Randy nodded. "But I didn't need to add to that. I know you love Donovan and worry about him just as much as I do, but I guess I always feel like it's my job to protect him."

"I know that too, Randy. I just can't sit back and have you attack

182

my best friend, especially when you know as well as I do that she's doing what she has to do. Donovan knows the risks he takes when he works a case like this. Sometimes the most dangerous criminals are cops themselves."

"You're right," Randy said quietly, and Joe knew she was remembering Dickerson. "And after our last fight about Donovan I promised myself I was going to ease up a bit. But this was a lot more than just a reprimand. I wasn't thinking clearly—all I could see was my worry for Donovan, and that things were hitting too close to home again."

Joe pulled her into his arms, stroking her hair. "I know. Me too."

Randy raised her head. His lips came down on hers, and she felt his arms tighten around her. They kissed for a long time, just enjoying each other. They were interrupted by the sound of shuffling feet.

Joe looked up. Rick was standing in the doorway, his grin wide. Randy looked around and saw him. She smiled slyly at him, and he smiled back.

"How's it goin'?" Rick asked, his tone indicating he already knew. "Ya know, you could actually leave on time for a change," he said to Joe, looking at his watch pointedly.

"I'm plannin' on it," Joe said, his grin wide, his blue eyes twinkling.

An hour later Joe and Randy sat in a restaurant having a quiet candlelight dinner. They talked about everything, and nothing at all. It was like getting back to where they were before Donovan's shooting, before the argument. By the time they left the restaurant, hand in hand, Randy felt like everything between them was restored. Joe was smiling as they walked over to his car. Once inside it, he leaned over and kissed her deeply. "This was great," he said, his voice low.

"Wait till I get you home," Randy said, grinning rakishly.

Joe nodded, his smile wide. "Uh-huh…"

Ten minutes later he dropped her off at her white Jaguar, still parked in the department lot. "I'll see you at home," she said, leaning down to kiss him again.

"Oh, yes," Joe said with a grin. "I'll follow you."

Randy nodded and got into her car.

The freeway was still fairly busy even for that time of night. Joe had a hard time keeping up with her. She was driving faster than normal, and he was amused to think she was in a hurry to get home. He was just thinking about calling her on her cell phone when he saw a flash of light, like sparks from metal meeting metal. Then the cars in front of him seemed to scatter, as if avoiding something. Joe slowed up, wondering what had happened, assuming correctly that there had been an accident. He sighed, knowing this could waylay him; if there were no other police on the scene he would be expected to help out until assistance arrived. He pulled off into the emergency lane and drove carefully up it until he reached the accident. He only knew it was the site by the cars pulled off to the side and the people standing at the top of an embankment looking down. "Great," he muttered as he threw the brake on his Porsche and climbed out.

Joe strode over to the people standing by. "Did anyone see what happened?" he asked, his voice official.

A woman holding a small child turned to him. "There was a van, a white one, and it hit that car and sent it over the embankment." She pointed with a small hand toward the car lying on its roof below them. Joe followed the line. It took him a long moment to realize that the car was a white Jaguar.

"Sonofabitch," he said as his stomach twisted into a knot. He ran headlong down the embankment, yelling over his shoulder for someone to call 911 and tell them an officer was down. He yelled Randy's name over and over as he reached the car, but she didn't respond. Throwing himself on the ground, he tried to look inside. The roof was crushed down, and since it was dark it was hard to see anything. "Randy!" he yelled, his voice strained. "Babe, come on, you gotta answer me!" He heard nothing.

Jumping up, he grabbed the door handle and started to pull—it didn't give. He yelled up to the people above, asking if anyone had a crow bar or something to pry the door with. After a long few moments, a man came running down the embankment with a bar in his hands.

Joe grabbed it and jammed it into the seam in the door, working it into it with the force of his worry and anger. Throwing all of his weight against the bar, Joe felt the door give slightly. He continued to shove against it until he could get his hands around the frame. Heedless of the metal and glass cutting into him, he curled long fingers around the window, and bracing one foot against the car he used all his might to pull at the door. It took three tries until it gave with a shriek of metal. The man who had brought the crow bar helped him shove the door as far out of the way as possible. Joe dropped to his knees to look inside. Randy lay unconscious against the crushed roof. Joe could see blood on her face and her chest. Steeling himself against the terror that kept threatening to rise up and engulf him, he crawled inside.

"Randy, babe," he said shakily, reaching out to touch her face.

185

He brushed her hair back and checked with shaking hands for a pulse. She had one, but he thought it seemed faint; he wasn't sure—his hands were shaking so much that he couldn't get a good reading. She had a cut on her forehead. Opening her blouse, he saw a deep wound to her chest. It was bleeding profusely and Joe could see that her breathing was labored.

Throwing off his jacket and pulling his shirt off, he balled up the garment and pressed it to the wound in her chest. "Hey," he said, glancing over at the man who had helped him with the door. "Do me a favor—run up to my car, and in the trunk there's a first aid kit—grab it for me. And make sure someone called the ambulance. Hurry!" His voice was strong and sure, even as every nerve in his body screamed at the idea that this was his wife lying there bleeding, and maybe dying. Stroking her hair, he waited for what seemed like hours. Finally the man returned with the first aid kit and told him the paramedics were headed down the freeway at that moment. Joe pulled away the shirt to check the bleeding; it seemed to have slowed, but it still hadn't stopped. He continued to apply pressure, pulling open the first aid kit with his other hand. Taking out a pressure bandage and ripping it open with his teeth, he pressed it to the wound on her head. The injury didn't seem as serious, but he wanted to make sure he covered all the bases.

Ten minutes later the paramedics were taking over, and Joe moved aside to let them get to Randy. He pulled on his jacket as the man who had helped stood by and watched the paramedics work. "You know her?" he asked Joe.

"She's my wife," Joe replied, his voice halting with the sudden emotions that were beginning to hit. His adrenaline was slowing down, and suddenly it was all getting to him.

186

It only got worse at the hospital. Randy was immediately taken into surgery, her condition listed as critical. Joe called Midnight, who was still at the office. She promised to make all the other necessary phone calls to inform his family.

By the time Midnight arrived at the hospital, Joe had been told that two of Randy's ribs were broken and that one had split outward, causing the wound Joe had treated; the other had punctured one of her lungs. Her condition was listed as critical at that time. When Midnight found him, he was pacing and smoking outside the waiting room. He'd quit smoking when the children were born, but now he needed something to occupy his mind. Midnight noted that he wore no shirt and he was shivering in the February night air.

"Joe, come inside, you'll catch pneumonia. Come on," she said, pulling on his arm. Joe tossed his cigarette down and allowed her to drag him inside.

Donovan arrived a few minutes later, his face drawn and worried. He and Joe hugged. Joe told him everything the doctors had said, and then repeated it when Darrell arrived. Rick came shortly after that, as did Spider, Tammy, Tiny, Jessica, Dave, and Kana. They were Joe's extended family, and when he was in a crisis, so were they.

They spent the next three hours waiting for the doctor to tell them she'd come through surgery. By this time, Donovan was doing a lot of pacing and Joe was sitting in a chair with an unreadable expression on his face. Midnight was on the floor next to Joe, Rick behind her on the chair next her best friend's, her right hand resting on Joe's leg, her left clasped in Rick's at her shoulder. The rest of the gang was there too, always present for their extended family.

The doctor came out and headed straight for Joe. Everyone

came to an alert position, waiting expectantly.

The doctor pulled a chair over to sit in front of Joe, his eyes scanning the other people waiting for the news as well. "Mr. Sinclair," he said, his voice business-like. "Your wife is out of surgery. As I explained before, her rib punctured her lung, and we've repaired the damage there. She has a concussion and a number of other minor injuries. Our main concern right now is the injury to the lung. That is what we will monitor for the next forty-eight to seventy-two hours. Right now I have her listed in critical condition. If she fares well tonight, I will upgrade that to serious condition. She'll be in recovery for a long while. She isn't responding to the medication we gave her to wake her up from the anesthetic used during surgery, and that is causing us some concern as well. I will keep you updated, but this will definitely be a long night. I suggest you all try to get some sleep."

The doctor glanced at the people around him, surprised that his patient had so many dangerous people worried about her. He left them then, and Joe glanced over at Donovan. He looked stricken, and Joe went over to him.

"You should go home for a while, Donovan," he said gently. Donovan started to shake his head, but Joe could already see what a toll it was taking on the younger man. "I'll call you as soon as I hear that we can see her. Okay? It won't do you any good, hangin' around here. You still aren't a hundred percent from your own time in this place."

It was true enough. Donovan had been overdoing it recently, working late nights and getting up early to start over again. He was trying to work through all of his aggressions and worries, and now to have to add this to his list of concerns…

It seemed like too much, and he felt the definite need for something strong to drink. After a long pause, he nodded slowly. "Make sure you call me though," he said, his voice a lot stronger than he felt. Midnight stood to walk him out to his car.

"She'll be okay, Donovan," she said.

"She better be." He turned to her. "What do we know about the accident?"

Midnight leaned back against the car parked next to Donovan's. "She was hit by a van, and the van took off. Some of the witnesses got a partial plate." She hesitated, not sure if she should tell him the rest. Rick had questioned some of the witnesses himself, and some of their answers had been disturbing.

"There's something else, isn't there?"

"Yes." Midnight nodded. "Some of the witnesses got the impression that the van hit her on purpose. They saw it move over three full lanes to get to her, even slowing down in front of her to try and make her pass them on the right. I don't know, Donovan—it has a familiar ring to it, ya know?"

"Like what happened to me—a setup." Donovan felt every muscle in his body tense at the thought. The bastards were trying to kill his sister now? Maybe they'd hoped the kids were in the car too…

"Shit, Midnight, the kids—where are they?" he all but yelled in his sudden panic.

"Relax, Donovan," Midnight said, putting her hand on his arm. "Christian is with them. He said he'll stay up at the house until we know what's going on for sure. He'll take care of them, don't worry."

Donovan nodded, blowing his breath out in relief. Whatever he had against Christian, he knew the man could be trusted to watch over Joe's children. Christian was nothing if not loyal to his cousin. After a long moment, Donovan reached out and drew his boss into a hug. "Thanks, Midnight," he said against the top of her head. "I'm glad Joe and Randy can always count on you and Rick and the rest of the gang to come through for them."

"It goes all the way around, Donovan. We're family, all of us." She pressed her hand to his cheek in a comforting gesture. "She'll be okay. She's a fighter. She'll come through this."

Donovan nodded, not entirely convinced but wanting desperately for her to be right. He drove home a little while later. Walking into the house, he headed straight for his kitchen. He poured himself a few shots of Goldschlager and Jägermeister, feeling the beginnings of warmth spread in him. He made himself a double, added ice, and headed into his bedroom. He kicked off his boots, pulled his badge off his belt, and took off his holster. He shrugged out of his jacket and sat down on the bed, nursing his drink. It was almost half past midnight.

At around one o'clock, Donovan was working on another double shot when the doorbell sounded. Reaching over lazily, he touched the intercom button. "Yes?" he asked, just a little too buzzed to be curious about the hour of this visit.

Serena's voice came over the intercom. "Pony, it's me. I've been calling you, but there's been no answer. I heard about Randy's accident. Pony?" she said again when he didn't respond. "Pony, can I come in?"

Donovan stared at the button, thinking about just ignoring her altogether. He wasn't in the mood to deal with her. Her indignation

190

at his not returning her calls, her sympathy over Randy's accident. Her assertion that she could make things all better. She couldn't—no one could.

"Serena," he said finally, his voice sounding strange in his ears. "Go home. I'm not in the mood for visitors, okay?"

"Pony…" Serena began chidingly. Donovan turned off the intercom, not wanting to listen anymore. It buzzed a few more times, but then stopped. He figured she'd given up. He drank down the rest of his double and walked to the kitchen for another.

An hour and a half later the intercom buzzed again. Donovan ignored it. It buzzed twice more, then stopped. Donovan leaned back against the headboard, closing his eyes, allowing the euphoric feeling of the alcohol in his veins full run of his mind. Suddenly he sensed someone in the room. He came to full alert, his eyes darting from the gun lying on his dresser to the person standing in the doorway.

It was Jeanie, still wearing her uniform. When Donovan said nothing, she walked into the room. "Donovan," she said quietly, her eyes searching his face. "I heard about Randy's accident while I was on my ride-along tonight. I came as soon as I got off shift…" She trailed off as she sat down on the bed next to him.

Donovan was staring at her as if not believing she was really there. "Why?" was all he said.

Jeanie winced at the pain in his voice. "I thought you might need me."

Donovan said nothing, just looked back at her for a long moment. He sat up slowly, until they were within inches of each other. Jeanie didn't know what he was thinking; she didn't know if he was about to tell her to get out, or if he was going to hit her. He surprised her by slowly leaning forward, resting his head on her shoulder. She wrapped her arms around him and felt him almost slump against her. His hands slid around her waist, and then it was as if he was drowning. He held her tightly, allowing her to pull him to her. She held him for a long time, stroking his hair and back. "She'll be okay, Donovan, she will," she told him, over and over.

After a long while, Jeanie leaned against the headboard, pulling him with her. Donovan lay against her, feeling a little bit better. Her strength comforted him. Eventually he fell asleep, the alcohol finally overwhelming him. Jeanie stayed right where she was.

When Donovan woke the next morning, Jeanie still lay against the headboard, holding him close. She was asleep, and Donovan watched her for a long time, then carefully pulled her down so that her head rested on a pillow. He imagined that the way she was sleeping wasn't comfortable. He glanced over at the clock; it was 6:30. He picked up his phone and called the hospital. He was told that Randy's condition hadn't changed, and that visitors were still not being allowed to see her. When he hung up, he saw that Jeanie was awake and watching him.

"What did they say?" she asked softly.

"Her condition's the same. I still can't see her." Donovan lay back down and pulled her close, feeling the need to hug someone.

Jeanie snuggled into his arms, wanting to lend her strength to him as best she could. After a long while, she glanced up at him. "I figured Serena would be here," she said, then instantly regretted bringing up his girlfriend.

"She would have been," Donovan said evenly, "if I'd let her in."

Jeanie looked at him for a long moment, then shook her head.

"You didn't let me in," she said finally.

A slow grin spread over his face. "Yes, but you let yourself in, didn't you?"

"So why didn't she?"

"Because I didn't give *her* the security code."

"Ah…" Jeanie looked down at their bodies so close together, even though they were fully clothed. "How's she gonna feel about this," she asked, her gesture taking them both in.

Donovan shrugged. "Don't know, don't care." In answer to the questioning look on her face, he said, "Jay, we broke up about two weeks ago."

Jeanie looked at him for a long moment, blinking as if not sure she'd heard him right, then lowered her head and rested against him again. They lay silently for a long time. Eventually they both fell asleep.

The night of Randy's accident was hard on everyone. Christian stayed in the main house. His nerves were on edge; something told him Rick's suspicions were right and that Randy's accident wasn't an accident. Susan had spent the evening entertaining the children. They didn't understand what was happening, but they noticed that Christian was keyed up and that their nanny seemed very upset; because of that, they were extra needy.

Later, after the children were finally asleep, Susan wandered through the house. Christian had already double-checked every window and door to make sure they were secure. Eventually she wandered past the room he had taken. Christian was lying on the bed, but he wasn't asleep. Susan pushed open the door, and he looked up.

The worry and fear on Susan's face made him hold his hand out to her. She came forward immediately, taking it and lying down next to him. Christian's arms curled around her comfortingly. "I'm sorry," Susan said tearfully. "I just, this is so awful, I don't understand why these people are doing this. I'm scared."

"Don't, Susan," Christian said soothingly. "You don't have to explain. I know." His voice was so close, so warm.

Susan nodded and rested against him, allowing herself to relax, her tears rolling unchecked down her cheeks as he stroked her hair, his lips against her forehead. She'd called Warren earlier in the evening to tell him about the accident, looking for some comfort. His response had been that he was sure Randy would be fine, but even if she didn't make it, certainly Joe would keep her on to take care of the children. His comment had been, "He'll certainly need you then, won't he?" He had sounded smug and oblivious to her concern. Susan had hung up with a sense of unrealism. Did he really think that was all this was to her, a job? Didn't he know how much she cared about Joe and Randy, about all of them? Hadn't he been paying attention?

It struck her as she lay with Christian that he seemed to understand without ever hearing her words. He didn't need explanations, he didn't need her to tell him what was aching in her heart right then—he knew. It was the strangest realization, that her lover understood her better than her fiancé, the man who was supposed to love her.

CHAPTER 6

Joseph Sinclair sat in the hospital. He was waiting for them to come tell him that his wife was dead, but they never came. Eventually he began to wonder if she would just slip into a coma and stay that way. His months in the hospital after his parents' accident so many years before played through his head. He remembered the sense of helplessness. His parents had been dead, there'd been nothing to do. His thoughts lingered on the overwhelming sense of loss he'd experienced when he found out they'd died, when he realized that he was left behind to pick up the pieces. Now, if Randy died… He couldn't even think about it clearly. She'd been the one to fill the void nine years before. She'd been the one to make him understand that his parents' death had made him who he was. It was Randy's words that had released the guilt and pain he'd lived with for years. And now, here she was lying in a hospital bed, maybe slipping away from him as he sat in a goddamned waiting room.

That thought drove him to his feet. He strode over to the nurse's desk, as Midnight, Spider, and Tiny watched. Everyone was staying in shifts; Spider had sent Tammy home, as Tiny had Jessica. Dave Dibbins had headed over to Joe and Randy's house to take over the watch from Christian, who had insisted he needed to go into the office that morning.

It was Saturday; Randy's accident had happened Thursday night. There had been no change in her condition. Donovan and

Jeanie had shown up at the hospital on Friday morning. Donovan had looked hungover, but it was obvious that Jeanie was there to support him. Many members of the "family" were happy to see her with him. There'd been a general consensus among the members of the original FORS unit as well as their spouses that Jeanie had been a good match for Donovan. Nobody had liked Serena; she was very obviously not a cop-type woman, she didn't like or understand cops, and therefore she'd been no good for Donovan.

Donovan and Jeanie had stayed for a good portion of the day on Friday. Jeanie had been excused from ride-along that night, so she'd gone back to Donovan's with him when they'd finally left the hospital. They'd yet to show up that morning. Midnight suspected Donovan had gone to the office to start trying to run the partial plate the witnesses had seen on the van that hit Randy.

Joe stood at the nurse's desk until the woman there looked up.

"I need to see my wife," he said.

"Sir," she began placatingly, "your wife is still unconscious. The doctor will let you know when you can see her."

"No," Joe said, making a cutting gesture. "You're not listening to me. I want to see my wife. Now." His tone was deadly serious, and the nurse noticed the glint of a threat in his eyes.

After a long moment, she nodded slowly. "I'll contact the doctor, sir. I'll have him come see you right away."

Joe nodded, moving to within a few feet of the doors to the Intensive Care Unit. He proceeded to pace in a tight line in front of them, throwing glances over at the nurse, telling her with his body language that if the doctor didn't show up, or didn't give him an escort to see his wife, he'd find her himself.

Midnight stood up and walked over to him. She stood at one end of the area he was pacing, and when he reached her, he stopped and looked at her for a long moment. It was a striking scene to everyone watching. Midnight was so small compared to Joe, but the way she stared up at him exuded a powerful message of support and concern. After a long moment, he reached out and hugged her to him. Her hand buried itself in his hair, pulling him down to her as she whispered something in his ear. Joe nodded against her shoulder, then straightened. Midnight turned and led him over to the couch in the waiting room. After a moment's hesitation, he lay down, having to bend his legs to fit on the small couch. Midnight sat down on the floor next to him. She stroked his hair as he closed his eyes. Neither of the men in the room seemed surprised by the action; they knew Joe and Midnight well enough to know that she was trying to hold him together, and would do whatever it took to keep him at least partially reasonable.

When the doctor arrived forty-five minutes later, Joe had slept just enough to be better able to reason with the man. He told him that he needed to be with Randy even if she wasn't awake. After a lot of deliberation the doctor said that Joe alone could go in to see his wife. Midnight told him that the rest of them would wait outside to hear anything.

"We'll be here," she said, her catlike green eyes focused on him as if she were trying to transfer strength to him. Joe nodded, then followed the doctor into the Intensive Care Unit.

The room he was led to was private, as per Joe's own arrangements. Randy's face was bruised, her eyes blackened. Joe felt physically ill at the sight. He'd dealt with much worse, with fellow officers, even Midnight being injured, but he'd never had to deal with Randy

197

being so badly hurt. The closest he'd ever come was when she'd had their children, but at least then he knew there would be a positive end to it all. Now he didn't know for sure what was going to happen. It drove him crazy to think that no matter how much they loved each other, no matter how much they'd been through, she could still die without ever regaining consciousness. He sat down in the chair next to her bed, taking her left hand in his. He stared at her wedding ring for a long time, remembering the day he'd bought it for her. They'd gone to the jewelers in London, his father's jeweler. They'd picked out the solitaire for the ring. Joe had suggested the blue topaz because it was the same color as her eyes. It was an exquisitely cut stone to which Joe had the jeweler add a number of perfectly cut diamond baguettes, set in the band and curving around the solitaire. To the engagement ring and gold wedding band, he had added a golden band set with blue topaz baguettes a few months before, on their ninth wedding anniversary.

Joe sat there holding her hand, waiting for something. He wasn't sure what. He silently prayed she'd wake up and tell him it had just been a bad dream.

But Randy didn't wake up, and he sat watching the monitors and lights blink, listening to them beep and buzz.

Donovan and Jeanie walked into Midnight's outer office and heard someone clicking away on a keyboard. Pushing open the door, Donovan saw Christian sitting at Midnight's computer. Christian turned around, noting that Jeanie stood just behind Donovan. He grinned and nodded to her, then looked at Donovan.

"I thought you'd be at the hospital," Christian said.

"I gotta do something, otherwise I'll go nuts," Donovan said honestly, far from in the mood to fence with Christian. "Where're the kids?"

"Dibbs is with them—they're safe," Christian said, understanding Donovan's concern.

Donovan nodded. "What're you up to?" he asked, squinting at the screen behind Christian.

The Englishman motioned them forward, gesturing to the computer. "Right now, I'm trying to come up with a quick way to search DMV's files for that partial plate the witnesses got."

Donovan was surprised that Christian was so involved already. "How's it coming?"

"Slow but sure," Christian replied. "Actually, your expertise might help some. I know you know DMV procedures inside and out—I could use that knowledge to help tailor the program better."

Donovan leaned against Midnight's desk, looking at the screen, then shook his head with a wry grin. "I don't understand a damn thing you have there right now."

Christian laughed. "That's because it's machine language right now. Once I have something noteworthy I'll show you what I'm trying to get it to do. What I could use is some examples to feed the system to work the run-throughs."

"Can I help?" Jeanie asked, coming to stand beside Donovan.

Christian nodded. "Yeah, you and Donovan can go pull me some plates with the partial in it. That'll give me the samples I need."

"You got it," Jeanie said, glancing up at Donovan. "Can you show me how to use the CLETS system? We haven't covered that yet in the academy."

Donovan looked at her for a long moment, then nodded. They walked back out into the outer office and he proceeded to show her how to access the Department of Justice system. Jeanie found that even in the current crisis, it felt good to have him so close again. He sat just behind her, reaching around her to show her what keys to use. She could feel his warmth at her back and couldn't help but think about two nights before; it had felt so good to be with him again. They hadn't kissed, or really touched intimately; they'd just lain together, but it had felt so good. Waking up in his arms each morning had been almost pure pleasure even with both of them clothed.

Jeanie was glad she had decided to go to him the night of Randy's accident. She hadn't been sure he wouldn't throw her out on her ear, but she knew she'd needed to at least try to be there for him. Knowing how much he loved his sister and hearing how critical her condition was, she'd been certain that Donovan would be in bad shape. She had meant it when she said she thought Serena would be with him; she had steeled herself against seeing them in bed together. When she'd arrived at his house, she hadn't seen any other car there but Donovan's. She'd buzzed the intercom a number of times, but when he didn't respond she got worried and used the security code he'd given her after he'd been shot. Walking in and seeing him lying on his bed, she'd been speechless for a moment. Even in his obviously inebriated state he had looked so incredible. But when he'd actually leaned on her, it had taken her breath away. She knew she had done the right thing by being there, and she was extremely happy she'd taken the chance.

After a while it became very obvious to all three of them that it was far too quiet in the office. Christian reached over and picked up the remote to Midnight's stereo system. He had to adjust the station to something more his style, then turned it up. All three of them listened as Matchbox 20's "Real World" played. They all sang the chorus, which said, "I wish the real world would just stop hassling me." It was how they all felt at that point.

The three worked together for the entire day. Finally, at 6:00 that night, Christian had his program ready to run. He entered the last bit of information and told the program to execute.

"It'll take all night to compile all the data DMV has. Tomorrow we can sift through the results," he said, standing up and stretching. He glanced over at them as they got up too. "I don't know about you two, but I need a fucking drink."

Jeanie nodded immediately, agreeing wholeheartedly. Donovan looked between the two, then nodded slowly. "Let me call the hospital first," he said, going over to Midnight's phone. He phoned, and was told that Randy's condition hadn't changed.

An hour later Donovan opened his door to Christian and Susan. Christian had called the house before leaving the office and found that Midnight and Rick's nanny had come and gotten the children. Midnight had felt safer with the children at her house for the moment, and she knew Christian would want to be able to go to the hospital to see Joe eventually. Christian had shown up at the house and taken Susan by the hand, leading her out to the black Jaguar. She'd surprised him by not protesting in the slightest. Jeanie, Donovan, and Christian had decided on buying liquor and consuming it where they were less likely to get into any trouble. Considering the tension that was gnawing at each of them, they figured they wouldn't be able to get into a big fight with anyone other than each other. Instead of fighting, however, they ended up talking and laughing, generally relaxed in that moment. At one point during the evening, Jeanie looked at Christian and Donovan sitting on the couch. Christian was wearing a black shirt with jeans; Donovan wore black chinos and a denim work-style shirt. She elbowed Susan, who was sitting on the floor with her.

"You know," she began, loudly enough for them to hear but as an aside to Susan, "if they got along better, they'd make a dangerous pair."

"How's that?" Christian asked, grinning at her, his eyes trailing over to touch on Susan's. She was nodding her wholehearted agreement.

"Well," Jeanie continued, pointing to Christian and then Donovan as she spoke, "you with your dark looks and light eyes, and Donovan with his all-American good looks and beautiful eyes, you'd be a killer pair. Women would just throw themselves at your feet."

"Ha," Donovan began, with a slight leer. "The question is, which one of us would get the better-looking women?"

"I only sleep with the best-looking women," Christian said, staring directly at Susan, a sparkle in his light blue eyes.

"Yeah," Jeanie said, with an indignant tilt to her head. "Well, the best-looking women seem to flock to Donovan, so…"

Christian laughed, as did Donovan.

Christian raised his glass, tilting it toward him. "When a very beautiful woman runs to your defense, what can I say?"

Donovan raised his glass and clinked it with Christian's, glancing over at Jeanie. Jeanie raised her glass to both of them, then downed her drink. They spent the rest of the evening in much the same way.

Eventually, Christian had to call a cab to take him and Susan back to Joe's. Once inside the house Christian went about verifying that it was secure. Susan wandered down the hall, feeling very light-headed from all the alcohol.

When Christian made his way to his room across the hall from Susan's, he found her lying on his bed with her eyes closed. He stepped inside, kicking off his boots and pulling his shirttails from his jeans. Lying down on the bed, he pulled her into his arms, looking down at her almost tenderly. Susan opened her eyes to look up at him. Without a word Christian bent his head and kissed her gently on the lips.

Susan sighed, giving herself up to the feeling of his lips, and he wrapped his arms around her. She clutched the front of his shirt with one hand, and the other found its way into his hair, entwining itself there. After a long kiss, their lips parted. Christian looked down at her, but still said nothing. Susan kept silent as well, not wanting to spoil the moment. She knew it drove him crazy when she started asking questions, or saying things he didn't need or want to hear. There was so much going through her head at that moment, but one thought swirled into very clear focus as she looked into his blue eyes.

She loved this man. The thought startled her. Did she really love him? He was incredibly, insanely handsome—God knew that was true. But he also understood her, he knew her. He excited her like no other man had ever done. He was so different than what he appeared to be, and she sensed that he could be the most loving man she'd ever met. She also knew that to tell him she loved him at this point would be an incredibly dumb thing to do. She'd heard his mantra about not believing in love, never had, never would. She also sensed how volatile he could be when he was backed into a corner, and telling him she loved him would certainly do that.

Instead of saying what was on her mind, she snuggled closer to him, sighing again. Christian tightened his arms around her, feeling unusually comfortable. It was the third night in a row they'd lain together, sleeping but not having sex. It was an unusual occurrence for him, with the exception of the times he and Jeanie had spent talking about Donovan and Susan, but even that wasn't like this. He and Susan weren't talking; he was holding her, and she was snuggling against him. It felt good, and that thought bugged the hell out of him. He knew he was getting too comfortable with her, and he knew how women tended to think. He knew that next she'd be getting all doe-eyed and thinking there was some romance there. Then he'd end up hurting her to keep her at a distance, like he had when he'd allowed her to walk in on him and Jeanie. He dreaded that happening, but he could already sense it as inevitable.

On Sunday, Jeanie and Donovan ended up at Joe's house with Christian at his computer. They were all hungover just enough to not want to drive all the way to the office again. Christian was able to pull up the results of his program search through the modem connection he'd set up with Midnight's computer. The list of possibilities he printed out was daunting, but it did help to narrow the search some. This way at least they didn't have to do it entry by entry. Christian was better able to narrow the results by showing only vans. The list was still large, but it gave them something to work on.

Jeanie had to return to academy classes Monday morning; Donovan drove her there. He spent the rest of the day at the office, working on the list. They purposely kept Christian out of the direct mix, in an effort to limit the amount of people actually working on "the case." It was Midnight's decision, and Donovan respected it, but Christian told him in an aside that he'd work on it with him at the house later. Donovan nodded, grinning conspiratorially.

Midnight was in the office that morning, having left the hospital for the first time in four days, other than to go home and check on Mikeyla and spend some time with Joe's children on Sunday. She'd taken time out to shower and change and had gone right back to the hospital as soon as the children were asleep. In many ways she was returning to previous experiences when Joe had been in the hospital. She spent her days keeping watch over him, now that they'd let more than one person in Randy's room. She stayed connected with the office and Rick through her cell phone, pager, and now laptop.

On this particular day, however, she was in the office, and shocking a lot of people; she was dressed to the nines, wearing a deep plum silk camisole under a cream silk suit jacket, tapered at her tiny waist. Her silk skirt accented her slim figure, cut to about three and half inches above her knees, exposing a great deal of silky-nylon-clad legs in three-inch cream suede strap-style pumps. A gold chain-link belt wrapped around her waist and dropped in a loop over her ever-flat stomach also accentuated her slim waist. She wore a gold watch and gold hoop earrings. With her ever-present tan, her copper-blond hair pulled up and away from her face with a pearlized clip, cream and plum eye shadow with plum liner accenting her catlike eyes and the perfect dusting of blush and lipstick that gave just a hint of color to her lips, it was a heady combination. Rick, who had left for the office long before she'd gotten ready that morning, just about dropped dead at the sight of her. He never got over what a beautiful woman his wife was, but on this occasion she'd managed to leave him speechless for a few moments.

The look in her husband's eyes told Midnight she'd achieved her goal. She had dressed to impress. Her confidence in her looks had everything to do with her husband's constant attention and his comments on her beauty. She grinned almost evilly at his reaction.

"I'd say I look okay, huh?" she said, a note of humor in her voice even in the current circumstances.

Rick's deep blue eyes swept over her from head to toe again, his mouth still hanging open. He nodded dumbly for a moment as his eyes met hers, then stammered, "I'd say you look incredible." He rolled his eyes heavenward, then looked back at her with mock seriousness. "Jesus, woman, didn't anyone ever tell you that you're supposed to become less appealing to your husband after nine years? I could drag you off to a hotel right now and make love to you for the rest of the day, given the chance."

Midnight grinned, her eyes twinkling at the thought. "Yes, well, you're not getting that chance, Mr. Debenshire."

"Big meeting today, huh?"

"Oh, yes." She rolled her eyes as she sat down at her desk.

Rick walked over, perching on the table in front of her desk. "City council, right?" Midnight nodded affirmation; Rick nodded too. "Uh-huh. So what are you gonna tell them?" He knew she was going to the council meeting with the demand that they give the officers in her department a raise. It had been seven years since the last one, and the officers as well as their union were getting very testy about the issue. Midnight knew if she couldn't do something soon, she'd end up with a "Blue Flu" epidemic, and she didn't want to think of the havoc that could cause.

Midnight looked at her husband for a long moment, as if considering what to tell him. Finally she leaned back in her chair, steepling her fingers together and giving him a pointed look. "I'm gonna tell them either my officers get a nine percent raise, or I quit."

Rick looked back at her for a long moment, surprised. They'd talked about the problem often enough in her two and a half years as chief, but she'd never actually said she'd quit if she didn't get what she wanted. Rick knew, however, that it was an effective threat.

The city council was extremely pleased with her work as the Chief of Police. Surprisingly, she hadn't managed to crush too many toes with her straightforward, not always tactful way of doing business. Fortunately, many of the council members thought of her as a breath of fresh air. She wasn't a politician, she was a cop—therefore she didn't play games, she didn't kiss up, and she didn't lie. They liked that. Especially the former Chief of Police for the San Diego Police Department, who had recommended her for the job with the complete backing of the Attorney General and Governor.

Midnight noted Rick's reaction and grinned sheepishly. "Guess that trust fund of yours might come in handy after all, huh?"

Rick nodded, his grin lopsided, his blue eyes twinkling. "Yep, that's what they said I'd end up doing someday, supporting you."

"Who's they?" Midnight replied, mockingly indignant.

"Oh, you know..." He waved his hand vaguely, then looked at her pointedly. "Everyone."

Midnight laughed, and Rick did too. He walked around her desk, and she stood to meet him. Even in her three-inch heels she was still four inches shorter than him. He bent his head, kissing her softly on the lips, sliding his hands around her waist to pull her closer. When their lips parted, he hugged her, his mouth close to her ear. "You do what you need to do. I'm behind you all the way," he whispered, then kissed her on the ear, and then on the neck, pulling back to look down at her.

"Even if I end up out of work?" she asked, staring up into his eyes, her smile wide.

He nodded. "Even if. I love you," he said, his voice soft and serious.

"Good thing." Midnight grinned, then stood on her toes to whisper in his ear, "I love you too, handsome."

"Yeah," he said, grinning back. "You say… Hell, I already got one comment about you this morning."

"And what was that?"

"Someone commented that you had the hottest legs…" He trailed off as she started to grin and shake her head.

"So what did you do?" she asked, knowing him well.

Rick shrugged nonchalantly. "I jus' told him that they wrapped around me perfectly."

Midnight laughed. Any other woman might have been offended by the remark, but Midnight knew that cops responded to that kind of comment. She knew Rick had been making a definite territorial statement to the officer and she suspected it had been quite effective.

A little while later Rick left her office. Christian walked in and dropped a printout on her desk, giving her a satisfied grin.

"What?" Midnight asked, narrowing her eyes at him. She began flipping through the printout and looked up at him in cautious amazement. "Is this what I think it is?"

Christian shrugged, leaning his hip against the table in front of her desk. "If you think it means that I've finished your inventory program, then it does," he said, his tone deceptively casual.

Midnight looked more closely at the printout, turning through the five-page document, scanning the layout and information it contained. She looked up at him when she got to the last page. "Are you telling me that you can capture all this information, but keep it formatted like this?"

Christian shrugged. "Yeah."

"And it'll look like this?"

"Yeah," Christian repeated, smiling now.

"I just thought... I mean, wow." Midnight was surprised and excited about the program he'd written. The format he'd put it in was both easy to read and high in content. It appeared highly polished, and Midnight was very impressed. She'd expected something crude and simple. Christian had come up with a way to capture the maximum amount of information with the minimum amount of clutter or complication.

Christian watched her, his light blue eyes taking in her amazement. He looked pleased with her reaction. "I take it this will do?" he asked finally.

"And how," Midnight said, laughing lightly.

"Now I need to do the grunt work part of it. I need to do the entry from the log books, and the current hard-copy inventory Jay and Donovan worked up."

"Okay…" Midnight said, her mind turning. "How long do you think it'll take?"

"Could take some time. You've got a pretty good-sized department here, Chief. I want to make sure I pick up everything. Then we'll have to recheck, and do a full inventory from that printout. But it'll be refined then."

"That will be a lot of work. How will we know what should be where?" she asked, daunted by the task.

"Well," Christian said, pursing his lips in thought, "I'm planning to record everything as being in the location it was last seen in. I've created a field that will list unit location. I'll be able to print out everything by location, by unit. Then you designate people to go and find that equipment, and then we know you still have it."

Midnight nodded, impressed again. "You've got a good investigative mind, Blue. I think you've got a good plan here. Thanks."

Christian smiled, happy with the praise—happier still that he had put so much work into the program to make it exceptional.

Later that day, Midnight was received with a standing ovation by her officers as she walked back into the office. Her bid for a raise had been approved, not before she'd told them she'd quit as the Chief of Police if they didn't. The city council knew better than to ignore her words. Midnight Chevalier-Debenshire did not make idle threats. She sincerely believed that what she was asking for was fair and just, and she fully intended to quit if she couldn't convince them of that. "You have the most beautiful city in the country," she had told them.

"You also have one of the higher crime rates in this country. If you expect these officers to continue to keep this city safe for tourist and citizen alike, then you need to pay them what is fair. Otherwise they'll just leave, and less dedicated and more poorly trained officers will take their place." She'd given them a pointed look then. "And you know what happens when you have poorly trained officers—shootings, mishaps, pursuit accidents. All of which spells big lawsuits and a lot of headaches."

When she'd left the meeting they'd voted seven to zero in favor of the raise. Her officers were overjoyed. Rick was extremely proud of her. He met her in the hallway on her way past the FORS office, grabbing her up in a hug and kissing her soundly.

"You did good, babe," he said, grinning widely. "Everyone heard about your threat to quit if they didn't give the raises. They were duly impressed."

"I didn't do it to impress anyone," Midnight said evenly.

"I know that, love," Rick said, touching her cheek gently. "But you impressed them all the same. Can't hurt your popularity around here."

"Tell me about it," Midnight said, finally breaking into a grin.

"You goin' to the hospital?" he asked as he started walking her to her office, his arm casually draped around her shoulders.

"Yeah, gotta make sure Joe's okay." She sounded like a worried mother suddenly. "He isn't eating much and he's hardly slept. If Randy doesn't get better soon, I think Joe'll be their next patient." Her tone was humorous, but the serious look in her eyes told Rick that she really was worried about her ex-partner. Any other husband would be jealous of the time she was spending keeping an eye on another man, but Rick was well aware of how important Joe was to Midnight, and he'd accepted it. After all, Joe was his best friend as well as hers. It was an odd relationship the three of them shared—Rick knew that, but it gave him comfort to know that Midnight would always be his wife and that Joe was always going to be someone else's lover and husband. Even after all that the three had been through together, and separately, there was still a slight tug at Rick's heart when he thought about the fact that Joe and Midnight had been a couple for a long time before he met her, and had had a brief yet important affair during Rick's and her marriage. He knew he'd never let anything like that happen again, and that it had in essence been his fault that she'd turned to Joe in the first place. But it was still a slight sliver of doubt in an otherwise perfect relationship. Rick figured it kept him on his toes, made him a better man, lover, and husband to her. In reality it was a good thing, but it didn't always appear that way.

Right now, however, Rick was as worried about Joe as Midnight was. She was right—Joe hadn't been eating, and when he did sleep it was in the chair next to Randy's bed in the hospital room. Overdoing it was a way of life for Joseph Michael Sinclair, but both Midnight and Rick knew what a toll it could take on his health. Rick offered to drive Midnight over to the hospital, and she agreed happily.

He glanced over at her as he drove. She looked very tired; he could see the strain her late nights and double time were taking on her. There were other ramifications as well. As if reading his thought, Midnight glanced over at him.

"How do you think Keyla is taking all this?" she asked.

Rick looked pensive for a minute, then answered honestly. "I think she's glad it's not you in that hospital bed."

Midnight looked surprised by his candor, but then nodded. "Yeah, I think you're right. This is rough for her…"

"It just shows her graphically what can happen."

"Yeah…" Midnight repeated, looking chagrined. "So what do we do?"

"I don't know," Rick said, shaking his head. "I don't really think we can actually *do* anything, can we? I mean, we can't quit, we can't stop being cops…"

"No." Midnight knew it was what he'd wanted her to do at one point, but also that he didn't think that way anymore. "I think the best thing would be to talk to her about what she's feeling, what she's worried about. We have to allay her fears as best we can, without being unrealistic."

"Okay," Rick said, grinning. He knew her bachelor's degree in psychology was coming out at that moment. She'd taken a number of follow-up classes over the years. She had become particularly interested in child psychology so she could better understand their daughter. Midnight had told Rick over and over that she had no intention of allowing her daughter to get as "screwed up" as Midnight thought she herself was. "You aren't like your mother was when you were growing up," had been his response to that. Midnight had known he was right, but she still needed to know she wasn't going to screw her daughter up like her parents had done to her and her brother. Rick knew how important it was for Midnight, and for that reason he reassured her constantly that she was a good mother, because he felt that she was.

There had been many times in the past few years when he'd come in to find his wife and daughter deep in conversation. When he walked in they'd grow silent, giggling incessantly when he questioned them about what they'd been discussing. It made him happy to see his family so happy. *His family*—the thought echoed in his head all the time. Midnight and he had come so far in the nine years they'd been married, yet they still loved each other just as much as the day they said their vows, probably even more. They understood each other better. They each knew the other's weaknesses, their joys, their sorrows, and what was important to them. It was a marriage based on a deep love, with a serious physical attraction thrown in, as well as a similar desire to make a difference in the world they lived in. They wanted to make it better for their daughter.

At the hospital, Midnight walked into Randy's private room. Joe was sitting in the same chair he'd been in for days now. He was holding Randy's hand, his thumb rubbing absently over her wedding ring. Rick watched from the doorway as Midnight walked over to her partner of over thirteen years. He watched as she reached out, putting a finger under his chin and tilting his face up so she could see him better. Joe's eyes reached her, and Midnight visibly flinched at the pain and worry in them.

"What's happened?" Midnight asked, her eyes searching his.

Joe swallowed, looking grim. "They said that there's an infection in her lungs. Probably from the external wound…" He trailed off, shaking his head.

Midnight knelt next to his chair, reaching out to hug him. Joe held her tight, shaking with the effort not to cry. "It's okay," Midnight whisper in her ear, as if sensing his reluctance to let his emotions go. At the sound of her voice, Joe did just that, letting out all the anguish, pain, fear, and worry that had been gnawing at him since the accident. Somewhere in the middle of it, Rick quietly left the room. He

214

knew that Joe would need Midnight for a while, and Rick himself felt a sharp pain in his heart at the sight of his friend in such distress. It reminded him of the accident Joe had been in years before, when his parents were killed. Rick walked outside the hospital, feeling the need to breathe the cool, crisp air.

Back in the room, Joe leaned back in his chair, and Midnight stayed next to him, winding her arm around his leg and leaning her head against his thigh. They were quiet for a long time, the clicking and beeping of machines the only sound in the room.

"What am I going to do, Night?" Joe asked quietly, his voice hoarse from disuse. Midnight looked up at him and saw that he was staring at his wife. After a long moment, he tore his eyes away from her and looked at Midnight. "What am I going to do if she dies?" There were tears in his eyes, and Midnight squeezed his leg.

"She's not going to die, Joe," she said confidently, as if that could make what she was saying true. "You two have been through too much and fought too hard to stay together for her to die now."

Joe gave her a wry grin that didn't reach his eyes. "You and I both know that doesn't have to mean shit."

"Yeah," Midnight said, her eyes narrowing slightly. "You're right, but I'll be goddamned if you're going to give up now."

Joe looked back at her for a long moment, then drew in a deep breath and blew it out again. He nodded slowly, closing his eyes. When he opened them, Midnight could see that he'd regained his composure. "Where are my kids?" he asked finally. He'd known Midnight would take care of that part of his world, so he hadn't worried. But now he felt like he needed something else to concentrate on.

"They're making the rounds," Midnight said, grinning. "They're spending time with Christian and Susan, some time at my house with Keyla and Marie, and then they've hung out with Donovan and Jeanie."

Joe looked surprised. "Donovan and Jeanie?" he repeated, his eyes lighting up just slightly.

Midnight grinned. "I guess she showed up at his house the night of the accident. They seem to be back together."

Joe nodded, his expression indicating that at least something good had happened while he'd been sitting at his wife's bedside. "So the kids are okay?"

"Yes, they're fine," Midnight said, smiling again. "By the time you two get out of here, they're going to be so spoiled you won't ever get them back to normal."

Joe grinned at that, his eyes trailing over to Randy again. "Just so long as we get out of here together," he said, his face darkening again.

Midnight nodded, then rested her head against his leg again. They stayed that way for hours. Eventually Rick wandered back into the room. He pulled a chair over to where they sat and drew Midnight up onto his lap. She leaned her head against his shoulder; it was obvious she was exhausted. Joe glanced over at the two, his expression melancholy. He was thinking about all that they'd been through. There had certainly been hard times for all of them. Between murder attempts, medical emergencies, infidelities, and just general mayhem, it had been an interesting nine years. Joe knew that whatever happened to Randy, he had to go on, even if he felt like part of him was dying at that moment. He knew he'd go on because of the children—if it wasn't for them... He closed his eyes against the pain that threatened to overwhelm him. He couldn't think of Randy dying; the pain was too sharp. The idea of having to go on without her was too much, and with the steely resolve that had gotten him through many things in his life, Joe turned back to his wife and sat quietly, waiting for her to wake up.

Seven hours later, things were much worse. Randy's breathing became labored and it was obvious she was struggling. Midnight and Rick had left by that time, and Joe was alone with her. She'd been breathing awkwardly for two hours. Joe had called the nurses in the minute it started, but they'd been unable to do anything and had sent for the doctor. Unfortunately things in the hospital were very confused and it was taking him forever to get there.

As Joe sat by nervously, Randy's eyes fluttered open. Joe was already holding her hand. He leaned forward, saying her name softly. She turned her head slowly, her eyes widening a little more at the sight of him. Her breathing was still labored, and it was obvious to Joe that she was in pain.

"Lie still, love," he whispered. "The doctor's on his way."

He trailed off as Randy began shaking her head. "No," she said, her voice a mere croak. "Please... need to..."

"What, love?" Joe asked, leaning down to hear her better.

"The children," she said, her voice clearer but still a whisper.

"They're fine, babe. They're with Susan and Christian." Again the shake of her head stopped him. "What is it, Randy?"

"Tell them... Tell them I love them," she said, her voice still halting as she struggled to breathe.

"You'll tell them when you come home," Joe said, searching her face.

"No, Joe. Tell them," Randy said, her voice becoming sharp as struggled to make him understand.

"Okay, okay, I'll tell them. You just lie there and rest."

But Randy was shaking her head again, tears coming to her eyes. "Love you, too," she said, looking up into his eyes.

"I love you too, Randy, and I'll tell you all about it later when we're home." But Randy shook her head at his pointed tone. Joe became almost frantic. He couldn't lose her now. "Randy, come on, babe, you can't give up now." But even as he said the words, her breathing seemed to become even more of an effort. She was staring up at him in something akin to fear, and Joe sensed that things were becoming dire.

A nurse walked in at that moment, and Joe's head snapped up. "Where the fuck is the doctor!" he roared. The nurse looked stunned, but then saw that Randy was awake and struggling for every breath. She ran out of the room.

Joe looked back down at Randy, bringing his hand up to stroke her cheek. Randy's hand came up to hold his. "Just hang on, love," he whispered. "Stay with me, Randy. Hold on."

His light blue eyes shone with unshed tears as he looked down at her. Randy's breathing became progressively shallower. The doctor arrived then, and he and two nurses went to work. One of them told Joe he should leave, but he shook his head, his face set in a determined line. "No, I'm staying with my wife." His voice brooked no argument and the nurse turned back to her work.

Joe had to move at one point to allow them closer to Randy, but he kept his hand locked in hers. When the nurse moved out of the way again, Joe leaned down, his lips next to Randy's ear. "I love you, Randy. Stay with me, babe. Don't leave me, don't go. Fight, please…" The last came out as an anguished sound, her eyes closing at the pain in his voice. Joe was fighting for her life, and he knew he was losing—it was tearing at his soul. "Randy? Baby, please don't leave me. I need you, I need you here with me. Please, fight…" Even as his last words faded, he heard her speak, so quietly he barely caught it.

"Love you…"

"I know, Randy, I know, and I love you," he said, kissing her cheek, his tears mingling with hers. It felt like an ending and Joe could barely stand the pain that was searing his heart.

It was at that moment he heard the worst sound in his life. The long, drawn-out tone of the monitor as her heart stopped beating. "Noo!" Joe yelled, as if that alone could bring her back. "No! Damn it, do something!" he shouted, his voice breaking. The doctor and nurses were working feverishly. Joe stepped back to lean against the wall, then slid down, bringing his knees up to his chest, resting his head on them and wrapping his arms around his legs. It took him a few long minutes to hear what they were saying.

"Sir? Mr. Sinclair, we've got her. She's back—sir?"

Joe's head snapped up as it finally sank in. He climbed to his feet and looked at the monitor; it was beeping again, as it had been for endless hours before. He watched it for a long minute while the doctor and nurses looked on quietly, as if he expected it to suddenly stop again. After a long moment, Joe closed his eyes, allowing the horror of what had just happened to drain away. Then he looked at the doctor, and the expression in his eyes said thank you a hundred times over, even if his voice wouldn't let him do so literally.

Donovan woke to the sensation that someone was watching him. Opening his eyes, he saw Jeanie sitting next to him on the bed, her eyes searching his face. He sat up.

"What's up?" he asked, his voice still husky from sleep.

"I'm just…" she began, but trailed off, her eyes moving over his bare chest, touching on the now healing scars on his shoulder and upper body. Without thinking, she reached out to touch the one on his torso. Donovan flinched ever so slightly. "Sorry," she said.

"It's okay, it's still just a little sensitive," he said, leaning against the headboard and giving her a quizzical look. "So you were just…" He allowed his voice to trail off as hers had, making her smile.

"I was just thinking about everything and wondering how things were going to turn out."

"In terms of what?" Donovan asked seriously, watching her eyes.

"Us," she replied simply, then shrugged to convey her confusion. "I just don't know where we stand anymore. And I know that's my fault, but I don't know how to fix it." She sounded anguished, and Donovan couldn't stop himself from touching her cheek.

"Jay," he said quietly, "things are just so crazy right now…"

"I know, and I don't want to ask you a million questions, because I know you're worried about Randy and you should be. I just… I'm sorry," she finished dismally, shaking her head.

Donovan grinned in spite of himself, pulling her into his arms. He held her for a long time, enjoying the feeling of her hair against his chest. Without stopping to think he nuzzled her head, and felt her lips against his skin. Putting his finger under her chin, he lifted her face to his. His lips came down on hers with surprising passion. Jeanie responded with equal fervor and within minutes they were locked in an unbreakable embrace. It took Donovan a long time to realize the phone was ringing. Grinning, their lips still touching, he reached for it.

"Hello?" he said, looking at Jeanie, who was still in his arms. As she watched him, however, Jeanie was sure she saw all the color drain from his face. She was alarmed at the emotions that played across his features. He was nodding, his eyes glazing over with tears. Jeanie touched his cheek, and he closed his eyes as he listened, swallowing convulsively. "Okay, but she's… she's okay now, right?" he said, his voice strained and agonized. He nodded again. "Are you okay, man?" he said, obviously worried. It was clear to Jeanie that the person on the other end of the line said he was, and Donovan hung up a few minutes later, leaning his head back with a deep sigh.

"What happened?" Jeanie asked, already having deduced that the call had been about Randy.

"She died, Jay…"

"What?" Jeanie exclaimed, but Donovan shook his head.

"They got her back, but… Jesus." He looked as if his world had crumbled from beneath his feet.

Jeanie could think of nothing to say. She pulled him into her arms, stroking his hair as he lay against her. One minute they'd been kissing, and the next she was as devastated as he was. She reflected on how she'd felt minutes before. They hadn't kissed since they'd been back "together." At least, everyone assumed they were together—

Jeanie didn't know that that was the case. But she knew Donovan needed her right now, and she was more than willing to be there for him. The moment they had shared just before that phone call, however, had reawakened all of the senses that he aroused in her when he touched her. She couldn't help but remember the times in bed with him before, the way he'd made her feel. His kiss had reaffirmed that he could still stir up the same myriad sensations. She wondered what the days to come would bring. She was very happy that Randy hadn't died; she hoped against hope that his sister would recover, but she didn't know what that would mean for her and Donovan. It was something that nagged at her, even as she held him that night. With all that had happened, with Donovan being shot and Randy's accident, things seemed to be getting dangerous. There was definitely blood in the water.

You can find more information about the author and series here:

www.sherrylhancock.com

www.facebook.com/SherrylDHancock

www.vulpine-press.com/midknight-blue-series

Also by Sherryl D. Hancock:

The *WeHo* series follows a group of women from Los Angeles as they navigate the ups and downs of love, life, work, and everything in between.

www.vulpine-press.com/we-ho

The *Wild Irish Silence* series. Escape into the world of BJ Sparks and discover how he went from the small-town boy to the world-famous rock star.

www.vulpine-press.com/wild-irish-silence-series